D. M. (David Morgan) Jones

Songs for the Hour

D. M. (David Morgan) Jones

Songs for the Hour

ISBN/EAN: 9783744770170

Printed in Europe, USA, Canada, Australia, Japan

Cover: Foto ©Andreas Hilbeck / pixelio.de

More available books at **www.hansebooks.com**

Mrs. Jeannette Lovell,

Compliments of the author,

David Morgan Jones.

May 31st 1905

Wilkes Barre Pa.

SONGS FOR THE HOUR.

BY

D. M. JONES.

PHILADELPHIA:
J. B. LIPPINCOTT COMPANY.
1896.

TO

MY LITTLE DAUGHTER.

WEE, golden-haired dreamer who knocks at my door
  With bright bits of fancy and Fairy-land news,
And now on your birthday, rejoicing at Four,
  With a four-leafed clover, to gladden my Muse!
Sweet enchantments of home! whose fairy and elf
  Lend their luck to the singer, and live in his songs!
The Queen of my fays is your fond little self,
  For now to the youngest the sceptre belongs.
Then come to my garden and smile on its flowers,
  And find that beforehand I wove you a crown
To wear on your birthdays, and brighten their hours,
  Reculling the roses they once rained down!

CONTENTS.

6　　　　　　　　*Contents.*

GWILYM GWENT.

THE COLLIER MUSICAL COMPOSER.

(Gwilym Gwent, the Welsh-American bard, was a household
word to every Cymro living, owing to the great popularity of his
inspiring musical compositions, which have swayed the Welsh
world for the past thirty years. He died suddenly on July 4,
1891, and was buried at the Hollenback Cemetery, Wilkesbarre,
Pennsylvania, where his friends and fellow-countrymen intend
erecting a monument to his memory.)

A TOILER awakened by voices divine,
A melodist sweet, too swart of the mine,
  And the chivalrous strife it inspires,
To forget in the glow of his song-breathing
      soul
The joys and the griefs of a cutter of coal,
  And his Motherland's emulous choirs!

Of blithe English rhythm he seldom lost sight;
But near the Welsh fountains of Bardic delight
  His music was more at its ease

When it merrily fifed for the soldiers of Toil,
Or unveiled the bright vistas of Beauty's own
    soil,
  When they echoed his star-lighted glees.

But wedded for aye to the rich Cymric tongue
Is his glee that the glories of Summer had sung,
  While it mirrored the smile of the morn,
Ere Ocean inspired the impassioned farewell
Of his harp to its home, under Liberty's spell,
  And the love-ties wherefrom it was torn,—

Its roof-tree that rivalled the cuckoo's retreat,
The *Eisteddfod*, in which he was wont to com-
    pete,
  Like the harpers and minstrels of old,
With his musical gems for the glittering prize,
Till they gleamed with the splendor of Cam-
    bria's skies,
  And the tale her grand symphonies told!

But his lyre, grown golden 'neath Liberty's
    dome,
More readily made fair Columbia its home,
  Since the song of the winds was the same
(Save jubilant chorus and conquering sweep)
Its Celtic strings caught from the voice of the
    deep,
  And the tongue that no tyrant could tame!

In the Arcady fairer than fancy had dreamed,
The meed of his music, the medals he deemed
  More precious than silver and gold,
Till the truth stared out of his toil-trampled
    ways
And song-waking wilds, that the mintage of
    praise
  Is worthless in hunger and cold.

When his heart was aweary of hammer and drill,
And melody rock-bound, with never a rill,

And fancy, with never a flower,—
When his longings divine were at war with his
lot,
In Nature's glad anthems his gloom was forgot,
Or poesy's soul-tuning power.

At work in the shadows disaster had spread,
In the death that is swift, and the sleep that is
dread
With the flame-swept mine in its thrall!
The music that comforts he caught from the
gloom
That had trembled so oft with the dirges of
doom
And Rescue's woe-fathoming call!

But grander the music he heard overhead!
And chalked by the light his mine-lamp shed,
In a trance on his uncut coal,
And traced on the mine door he tended at last,

When he seized, by the gates of a Hymn-
     glorious Past,
  The harp that still suited his soul!

Culture's charmed circle too shy to come near
A toiler as tuneful of soul and of ear,
  As if idolized all his life long;
Too content with his sphere? yet true as a star
To the key-notes of Nature, though singing so
     far
  From the centre of light and of song!

But a light has gone out in the Nottingham
     mine,
In Wyoming, a lamp that will nevermore shine
  Through the ripples of laughter and tears
That mingle in melody's beautiful tide;
The toiler has vanished who dreamed by its
     side,
  Entranced with the Song of the Spheres!

And Music, his true love, leads the vast throng
Who follow his hearse with victorious song,
  In his mother-tongue tearfully sweet,
That gives, as his anthems reverently gave,
The glory to God, when it bursts o'er the
      grave
  Where Beauty and Melody meet!

THE CELTIC ALLIANCE.

Long live the Race Alliance grand in Free-
    dom's battle formed,
When side by side the Celtic Three the heights
    of Home Rule stormed;
When gallant Gael the glances kind of Scot
    and Welshman cheered,
And the ancient race-love of the Celt in splen-
    dor reappeared.

Promise of Hope's fair angel! From the mo-
    ment of thy birth
A strange enchantment swept the seas and
    glorified the earth.
And this unmatched Alliance means the Celt
    the world around.
Then is it strange such rapture rose from that
    far battle-ground ?

After the battle, like the skies with all their
stars restored,

Free souls, a countless host, smiled on your
cause with one accord!

Men vied with men in Erin's aid, proud Celts
from sea to sea,

And Erin's foes began to ask why she should
not be free.

O deathless League, whose smiling cheer sore
chafed the victor's soul,

And made them seem the conquerors who
came so near the goal,

Your love and courage still remain, though
shadows gloom the day,

Not yet so dark from dauntless Celt can chase
the smile away.

Not yet so dark they may bedim that matchless Saxon's smile,

The England of the masses moves to aid the
    Emerald Isle,
The Grand Old Man of Celt-like soul this
    league of love inspired
That sprang to being at a bound when Free-
    dom's cause required.

While he the Gaelic column leads, whose quiet
    word means more
Than all the sway and grandeur of the Irish
    kings of yore;
His force intense, so self-contained, the face
    unchanged as fate,
Discerns fair Freedom in the dark, her hand
    on Erin's gate.

Right merrily, resistless League, your ranks
    again ye form,
Stern inch by inch to hold the ground, or take
    the field by storm,

While gallant Gael the gleefulness of Scot and
    Cambrian cheers,
And the ancient race-love of the Celt more
    splendid still appears.

The Thistle pricks Oppression's sides, the Leek
    is lit with smiles,
To greet the Shamrock growing wild o'er all
    the British Isles,
Where Celtic harps in chorus grand the tyrant's
    dreams disturb ;
And now 'tis Erin's Saxon friends he strives in
    vain to curb.

While Cheshire's freedom-kindled flame with
    Glasgow's glory blends,
Your Saxon allies' footsteps sound,—fair Erin's
    English friends.
Their swelling numbers moved and swayed by
    Truth's majestic might,—

The storm, a hand-breadth at the first, that
  smites the brow of Night.

In vain the foe the Gael proclaims,—the tide he
  cannot stay;
The outlawed Celt in your embrace grows
  dearer every day;
But when the Saxon joins the Gael, and courts
  the self-same ban,
Behold! A still more glorious league,—the
  Brotherhood of Man!

What friends of freedom are not proud to lend
  Old Ireland aid,
Who see what soul on Irish soil her children
  have displayed!
The heart for home all things endures till heart
  alone is left,—
The heart, still cleaving to the Right, of all its
  rights bereft!

Resistless Erin, conquering first thy friends and
    next thy foes,

No outlawry can reach the arm the world
    around thee throws;

And never worthier seemed thy sons of free-
    dom's sacred trust,

As with proud scorn they face the false accusers
    of the just.

In the bright blaze of Celtic fire forth-flashing
    for the Right,

The deathless Gaelic diamond emits a brighter
    light,

While tremble in the softer rays of its unsullied
    sheen

The fondest tears for Freedom shed the world
    has ever seen.

With Erin's songs by thousands sung outside
    the palace door,

And three crossed swords athwart his dreams,
    the tyrant's heart is sore.
Now lo! his own, nay, England's sword, the
    burnished sword of Right,
Discarded long, has joined the Three, and leads
    them in the fight.

What though the foe in fury charge, more des-
    perate than of yore,
Now let the battle-square be formed, for Erin's
    friends are four.
The England of the masses wakes,—the fight
    ye needs must win,
Defensive here, aggressive there, to hem the
    tyrant in.

While Cheshire's sacred firebrand the flame
    still farther sends,
The England of the masses comes! Fair Erin's
    English friends.

The Grand Old Man still grander seems.   Im-
    prisoned Erin thrills,
While Home Rule, like the cannon's boom,
    shakes old Britannia's hills.

September 2, 1887.

JOHN BOYLE O'REILLY.

From the hope forlorn that he led in his
    youth,
    There flowered in Liberty's light,
And the heavenly flash of the sword of truth
    That he handled for God and Right,
The legions of Liberty's grandest crusade,
    Where her standard was first unfurled!
And if Freedom must fall where her Charter
    was made,
    What hope for the rest of the world?

O heart, whose revenge for the wrongs of the
    past
    Was the love of his fellow-men;
The heights that he reached where his lot was
    cast,
    And the weapons he wielded then!

Columbia's fond looks for the Emerald Strand,
  Whose love-knot his own love had tied;
Home Rule's larger army he came to com-
    mand,
  And her ships on the waters wide!

But this was the key to his kindly heart,—
  The crown of his Celtic soul,—
That he prized not his land or his race apart
  From humanity as a whole.
Yet his love for a land was truer than theirs
  Whose affection is fixed on their own;
As the myriads of friends that he made un-
    awares
  Imagined he loved them alone!

His helping hand was an angel's wing,
  A giver who gave from choice—
Oh! here was a heart an anthem to sing,
  The spiritual strength and voice!

He pictured the crown in the workmen's tears,
  When their teacher was taken away;
And he filled his place through the busy years,
  And they wept on his burial-day.

When his bow for the brave Crispus Attucks
    he drew,
  With the love of humanity strung,
To the key-note that fell from the shafts as
    they flew,
  Was a song for the centuries sung!
And the song was a sword, for the Right
    withheld,
  Purpling Oppression's shield;
To his fairest true, like the knights of eld,
  Wherever the foe or field!

With a vision broad as the years to be,
  And as reverent of Liberty's shrine
As the Pilgrims who wandered from sea to sea
  In search of the treasure divine;

From their garlanded glory he cast the dead
  flower,
  With fadeless ones filling its place;
And sounding the note of our national power,
  Sang the hope of the human race!

Great of soul and of mind, and glorious of
  mien
  When he smiled in the leader's place;
In the shadows, sweet Pity's diviner sheen
  Endearing his patient face.
Thrice-conquered grave! where the life-shadow
  falls,
  And love is the sheltering tree;
Harp, sword, and cross,—his coronals,—
  And flowers from both sides the sea!

Flowers from a thousand valleys fair,
  Borne thither on sorrow's tide;

And the shamrock from over the sea is there,
   And the soldier is satisfied.
But his deeds still live, and will live more and
      more,
   Be fruitful and multiply;
For his like shall be seen on every shore;
   For God will not let him die!

October 10, 1890.

THE FLAG OF THE STARRY EYES.

(Read before the Conyngham Post, G. A. R., in Music Hall,
Wilkesbarre, Decoration Day, 1890.)

THE Flag that smiles, like the morning star,

   In Liberty's rosy gleam,

And nobly fulfilled, on the night of War,

   Her defenders' fondest dream!

Her mingling rays but the ripples are

   Of an in-rolling sea of light,—

Grander afloat in the blue afar

   Than she was in the soldiers' sight!

To be deemed forever diviner yet,

   In the peace of expanding skies,

In the pomp of a sun that shall never set,

   And the sweep of her starry eyes!

26

She has comforted them who moaned in the
   night,
   Their rivers of blood beside;
And her smiles were the stars that fought in
   the fight
   Which Freedom has glorified.
There is no sorrow she has not seen,
   No night to her gaze unknown;
And thus she has made, 'neath her smiling
   mien,
   The griefs of the world her own.
Outriding the storm on her radiant wings,
   And the shafts of the warring skies,—
'Tis a fadeless rainbow that Liberty flings
   'Neath the Flag of the Starry Eyes!

The colors we fly but the shadows are
   Of a Flag that is never furled!
The reflected rays of the morning star
   That is watched by a waiting world!

The beautiful herald, with glowing brow,
　　Of sunbeams that never despond,—
Of a sun that, climbing its zenith now,
　　Smites the darkness that lies beyond,—
The midnight dense or the misty deep,
　　Where the dew of the morning lies,
Or where men dream, in a troubled sleep,
　　Of the Flag of the Starry Eyes!

The ocean-path were a weary way,
　　And the sea a songless wild,
If the Flag of the Free, like the break of day,
　　On its billows had never smiled!
There is no triumph she has not won,
　　Worthy the brave to win ;
No gate-way of glory under the sun
　　That she shall not enter in !
Foremost to follow the Light above,
　　The grandest banner that flies—

In the regions of conquest or realms of love—
Is the Flag of the Starry Eyes !

She has led the brave, who were hers and ours,
Through the rugged ways of War,
To the soldiers' realm of unfading flowers,
Where she is the morning star !
Where the rosy shadows her folds let fall
Outrival the gifts of May,
And the garlands we bring at the bugle-call
For the dead who are hers for aye !
When its river of tears has emerged from the
gloom,
And the last fond murmur dies,—
Lo ! the river of fame, with its banks a-bloom,
And the love of her starry eyes.

She has won her way through the rayless pall
Of a valor that vied with ours;

With the kiss of forgiveness for one and all,
   Where Glory had scattered flowers;
Where the living have pledged her the death-
     less fame
   Of the dead whom they still adore,
Henceforth to be freemen in more than name,
   And to love her for evermore.
And which is the greater, their love who lost,
   Or ours, where the victory lies?
'Tis enough both belong, whatever the cost,
   To the Flag of the Starry Eyes!

Hers was the gaze of the soldier and seer,
   And the Truth it was grand to defend;
The vow, and the vision divinely clear,
   That the Union shall never end.
Reflecting the wisdom we all revere,
   And the glory to come in the end,
Hers was the glance of the soldier and seer,
   In the face of humanity's friend!

In the freedman's faith and the love of the
free
The proof of her greatness lies,—
Humanity's friend, on land and sea,
Is the Flag of the Starry Eyes!

THE HARP OF O'CAROLAN.

I.

THE WELCOME.

FORTH of a silence weird and olden,
But for her tears had been all golden,
  Whose cup of sorrow overran;
Tuned to the heart-beats of her bosom,
Who, smiling, sees her hopes in blossom,
  They bring the Harp of O'Carolan
  And they sing us the songs of O'Carolan!

Taken from Sorrow's weeping willows,
To catch the spray of briny billows,
  Those tears of joy space scarce can span;
Wakened by sea-winds westward blowing,
Till all thy golden chords are glowing
  With the heart and soul of O'Carolan,—
  Thrice welcome, Harp of O'Carolan!
  32

Kissed by the sunburst round thee clinging,
Proud of the shamrock, with it bringing
　　Hope for the universal man,
Come, Harp of Innisfail, the fearless,
And fill the eyelids of the tearless
　　With the righteous wrath of O'Carolan,—
　　With the joyous tears of O'Carolan!

In the New World's harbor kindly greeted,
Where Music's soul is never cheated
　　Of one sweet charm by blight or ban;
Thrilled with the strange and strong emotion
That sways the soul this side the ocean,
　　Thrice welcome, Harp of O'Carolan,—
　　The songs and the soul of O'Carolan!

II.

THE FAREWELL.

Farewell, brave Harp, to her returning
For whom unnumbered hearts are yearning,
　　Whose cup of joy too soon o'erran;

c

Oh! if there be the least despairing
Or drooping in her glance or bearing,
　Comfort her, Harp of O'Carolan,—
　Kindle her courage, O'Carolan!

Lift up thy voice so lark-like loud,
So clear, despite the passing cloud,
　A friendly sky she still may scan;
And, looking up, cease not to see
The golden sun of Liberty,
　That kindled the soul of O'Carolan,—
　The songs and the Harp of O'Carolan!

Harp of the brave, on Freedom's height
We heard, with hers attuned aright!
　Refuse the fires of hate to fan;
But be a fountain, cool and sweet,
Amid the conflict's torrid heat,
　For thou art the Harp of O'Carolan,
　And the song is the song of O'Carolan!

Lest her songs be sung by slavish rote,
The passion native to thy note
  Lose not, echoed from clan to clan!
Be strains like thine the heavenly vent
And healing of her discontent;
  While calm-voiced Patience steadies the van
  Of her conquering cohorts, O'Carolan!

July 23, 1885.

THE LIGHT OF LIBERTY.

ALL lights which were good in the eyes of the
  Lord,
  All lights that are sweet to the children of
  Eve,
Converge in her candle, whence issues a sword
  That flames without favor, and smites without
  leave!
And whether the wound be a smile or a tear,
  The truth disenthralled, or a lie laid bare,
We welcome her woundings, and hold doubly
  dear
  The Hand that is fearless, the Face that is
  fair!

Her sword is the sunshine ineffably bright,
  That kissed, as akin, the keen swords of our
  sires,

When the cry in their clanging was, "Let
there be Light!"
And the flash of their blades coaxed her
flickering fires.
'Tis the sword she presented her peerless defenders
Who had come to befriend her from over the
sea—
How her lamp has been burnished! And ah!
with what splendors
Its flame has been fed by the love of the free!

Freedom, whose lamp is half love and half light,
Yet not the least wanting in either of these,
So thy beauty blaze full on the world's ravished
sight,
Turn the light that is love t'ward the sorrow-
ing seas!
More hopeful their grief, and the storm's thrill-
ing story,

4

Than the silence that mocks, and the mirage
  that creeps.
Smite, rays that are sword-like, reflecting her
  glory,
  The dim lands beyond, where the love of her
    sleeps!

All lights which are good in the eyes of the Lord,
  All lights that are kind to the children of Eve,
Converge in her candle, whence issues the
    sword
  Which smites without anger, and flames with-
    out leave!
And whether the world she enlightens is
    wounded,
  Or the Darkness of Eld that would hold her
    in thrall,
The joy of the one, as she heals, is unbounded,
  And the shame of the other foreshadows his
    fall.

ERIN'S SWEET DREAM.

FREE skies shall yet cover her,—never despair!
　Lo! the tear-bursts that fall on both sides
　　the sea!
Free highways, free byways, for Erin, the Fair!
　Fear not for your fairy-land, Erin, the Free!

O Erin, the fair, whose fond heart were forlorn
　If bereft the sweet dream of Erin, the Free!
Sad mother! of thee are the merriest born,
　And the eyes all agleam with thy glory to
　　be!
All aglow with that dream with its rest and
　unrest,
　As real as the wrongs of the Emerald Isle.
Fair dreamer! sad mother! thy dream has
　been blest,—
　The tear owns its magic as well as the smile.

'Tis more than a dream, as the morning is
    more,
  When her weeping is all she may share with
    the night.
'Tis a waking to find the one friend at the
    door,
  Whose presence, in slumber, had gladdened
    the sight.

Bright dream ! on whose face fell the last
    blushing ray
  Of the sunset of freedom on Erin's fair shore,
Like the lone evening star in the footprints of
    day,
  It gleaned of the sunlight entrancing of yore,
'Mid the mists and the purple that mantled her
    skies,
  Through the cloud-racks, that rose with the
    turbulent years,

Down that splendid expanse where her chief
glory lies,
 Till it sounded the depths of the river of
 tears;
Where its silvery shadow was studied betimes
 By the king and his nobles, its beauty that
 praised,
But were wroth when they fancied 'twas Liberty's chimes
 Pealed over the tides as they brightened and
 blazed!

But ah! 'neath the frown and the frenzy of
wrong,
 And the tempests of terror that tyranny
 brewed,
It passed into proverb, and burst into song,
 That the proud soul of Erin could not be
 subdued!

4*

When hope feebly throbbed in the gathering
    gloom,
The longing that kindled that vision so fair
Kept the hearth-stone ablaze and the hill-side in
    bloom,
    That a glimpse of her Free Land might still
        glitter there :—
Wrote her legends of blood and heart-rending
    doom
    O'er the dust of the martyr, in memory
        deep,
That the Sunburst of Erin may find out his
    tomb,
    The firebrands of freedom illumine his sleep!

Oh, deathless desire! unquenchable dream!
    Love of liberty, shining in Liberty's stead!
The star of the eve in the morning shall gleam,
    When the pomp of oppression has faded and
        fled,

When the hopes that deceive her, the lights
that misled,

No more may distract when they cease to
beguile;

When all her waste places and hearts that have
bled

Shall be robed in bright raiment and win
back the smile!

When . winter, whose hardships were lightened
by wit,

And that glorious old king-scathing tongue
in the blast—

His snow-realms too oft by the death-candle
lit—

Shall voice the enchantments of freedom at
last!

Pale flame! burning heart,—outlasting the night,—
That will brook no requital save morning's
alone!

Shine on, sanguine fires, the lands that ye light
  Are all the fair dreamer may yet call her
    own ;
Fade not till the day come ! ye've conquered
    the might
  Of soul-stifling storms none but Erin have
    known ;
Outlasting the havoc of bailiff and blight,
  The hunger and heartache, the madness and
    moan ;
Surviving the grief, like a rose newly blown,
  As if lit in a garden of endless delight,
To melt in the smile, when the shadows have
    flown,
  Of that ruddy Aurora, the Eros of Right !

Deathless dream ! flashing scorn of the scaffold
    and cell,
  And sacred with sufferings for liberty's
    sake !—

'Twas Erin's fond glance on the exile that
fell

When that star shed its balm on the heart
that would break

But for Erin! who saw not the tears of her
son,

And, if seeing, had bidden him put them
away,

That her fight 'gainst oppression might sooner
be won,

As the death of her heroes had hastened the
day;

That her battle for home rule, for honor and
home,

May coax freedom's kiss to that gem of the
sea!

And her sons need no more brave billow and
foam,

In search of that fairy-land, Erin, the
Free!

Brave hearts to defend her, that never despair,

　Free lands to befriend her on both sides the

　　sea,—

The dream is from God! His smile it doth

　wear,

　Forecasting the twilight of Erin, the Free!

December, 1884.

BETWEEN THE SOWING AND THE REAPING.

THE sower's song is gay and blithe,—
  The blade appears; but while he's sleeping
Success or Ruin whets his scythe,
  Between the sowing and the reaping.

He finds them wrestling in the corn;
  Sometimes they stand together, weeping,—
The changeful Night, the fickle Morn,—
  Between the sowing and the reaping.

'Tis true we reap as we have sown,—
  That is, in kind; but in God's keeping
The blessing is, and His alone,
  Between the sowing and the reaping.

Yet some who cry "Our God is good,"
   Their harvest wains with plenty heaping,
Did all against Him that they could
   Between the sowing and the reaping.

And some who curse the God above,
   Amid their barren cornfields weeping,
Declared with fervor "God is love,"
   Between the sowing and the reaping.

But Faith, from Famine's withered breast
   To life miraculous upleaping,
Counts that abundance God has blest
   Both in the sowing and the reaping.

October 7, 1886.

LIGHT-HEARTED.

THE whippoorwill's call sounds blithesome to
    me
    As the bobolink's key-note of gladness;
My honeysuckles breathe, as they harbor the
    bee,
    Not the least hint of heartache or sadness.

My roses are ruddy and ready to look
    Death full in the face without sighing;
Not a flower in my garden that darkens its
    nook
    With dreams of the hardship of dying!

The daisies I love do not lavish their gold
    On the mounds where the dreamless are
        sleeping;

c   d   5   49

My violets hide not their leaves in the mould
  Where the long grasses weep with the weep-
    ing.

My lilies make ready by night to attend
  The Earth's golden wedding with Morning,
And a myriad fair things quaint offerings send
  For my Lord and my Lady's adorning.

It has cost me no tears to return you the kiss
  That comes with good-night and good-mor-
    row.
Light-hearted! Yes, dear, but is not your bliss
  Color-blind to the signals of sorrow?

THE LOVER'S IDEAL.

THE fairest flower that lifts her head
　To drink the dews that fall so free
Sinks gently down upon her bed,
　At night, my Love, to dream of thee.

The stars come out to give thee light
　And throw their radiance round thy form,
As though no other maiden bright
　E'er lived whose lips with love were warm.

The angels hover o'er thy path
　With tenderness and love untold,
And, with the heart an angel hath,
　Their arms about thy spirit fold.

They gaze upon thy beauty till
　They think of Eve before she fell,

When through their bosoms swept a thrill
  Of love and joy ineffable!

While flowers below and stars above,
  And angels sweet your presence deem;
May you fulfil, in life and love,
  My steadfast heart's more heavenly dream!

ONE OF LONGFELLOW'S LET-
TERS.

"I WOULD praise them more, had you praised
    me less"
Is a flower from his Muse, enfolding for aye
Its coveted secret in rosy duress,
    In a letter whose kindness is clear as day,
Revealing the grace and fragrance divine
Of a heart-flower of his for a handful of mine.

More precious to me was the praise implied,
    And the thorn thereof, than the praise ex-
    pressed;
For my heart, I trow, was more fit to be tried
    Than its tribute was by his friendly test,—
Discerning the dew on flower and thorn,
And the blush of the splendor whereof they
    were born!

5*

In the smile, I fancied, his letter reflected

  And flashed in the face of my love-smitten

    Muse,

A faint gleam of humor my fond glance de-

    tected,

  Yet not the least glimpse of it willing to

    lose!

But it symbolled the span—'twas the poet's last

    year—

From friendship's first smile to its farewell tear!

Even thus are the poets repaid by the Muse

  With one living line or one deathless lay

(And richer the meed she is loath to refuse

  Than that she bestows in a warm-hearted

    way),

From the happy Bohemian upholding her

    throne

To the prince who is king in a realm of his

    own.

Her favoring glance but a transient gleam

   For the many, a deathless smile for the few,—

Or a bosom friend, or a beautiful dream,—

   She rejects no lover because he is new;

But replies, when his rhapsodies run to excess,

"I would praise them more, had you praised

     me less."

May, 1892.

FAIR WYOMING.

Sing not, my Muse, as if in love wert crossed,
Of beauty's wane and beauty's battle lost.

Christened with joyful tears in verse divine
That flowed, a poet named her "Fair Wyo-
    ming;"
Whose lovely bowers were beauty's very shrine,
Which he at once, with rapturous outbursts fine
And farewells fond, still echoed in the gloaming,
Enshrined in song, and glorified Wyoming!

When from her Indian first love she was won,
Her brave white lover whispered, "Fair Wyo-
    ming!"
In the fond way he wooed her was it done;
In flowering field at rise and set of sun,

In forest din all day, and flowerless loaming,
While many a flintlock flashed for fair Wyo-
     ming.

Not without sorrow did he win his bride,
Herself a child of sorrows, fair Wyoming;
Not without glory, when their tears were dried
In Freedom's after-smile and patriot-pride,
Whence falls a tender light, for meet illuming
Of her remembered beauty, fair Wyoming.

She lifts her woodlands like a crown, but dotes
Upon her dappled dingles, fair Wyoming!
From Campbell's Ledge the vale-queen's ban-
     ner floats,
Hymned by the birds in blithe and plaintive
     notes,
Glad for the bonny realms banned not from
     blooming,
And sad for beauty blighted in Wyoming.

Chief of her splendors,—hint of golden hair,—
Falling from head to foot of fair Wyoming,
The blushing sunset's favorite river there,
A drifted dream of all that's bright and fair!
Ah! back to Gertrude's day is Fancy roaming?
Or dreaming? Fleeting glimpses, fair Wyoming!

She is not here nor there, the valley sprite,
Her foot-falls, free, elude us, fair Wyoming!
On hills which hide their hoarded wealth from
        sight
She sets her royal signet, daisy white,
Forget-me-not, and dandelion looming,
Queen of the wild-flower land of loved Wyo-
        ming.

The resurrected shine of suns long dead,
Clad in dark cloud and rainbow glow in glooming,
Casts a weird grandeur where their shadows
        spread!

For flaming flower the flowering flame instead,
That brightest blooms for Labor's sake consum-
    ing;
And oh! what sunbursts slumber in Wyoming!

Lo! in the dusk their shattered diamonds make,
And green-eclipsing cloud, for fair Wyoming
Plead many a pretty knoll and blooming
    brake
And little dewy dell, for beauty's sake!
While wooded hills, where glimmers endless
    gloaming,
Uplift their bannered green for fair Wyoming!

To hidden fields, 'midst lightnings harvested,
And caverned night's awakened thunders boom-
    ing,
The torch-plumed reapers brave are charioted
Adown the dark, while Doom's own shadow,
    Dread,

Flees from before their gay and fearless com-
    ing,
Who left their loves in care of fair Wyoming.

Night's roaring towers, day's phantoms dark that
    frown,
But share industrial grandeur's wonted gloom-
    ing,—
Wizards, that rain the rock-reaped jewels down,
And breaking them in sight of all the town,
Pluck from the fossilled leaves of Time's en-
    tombing
The golden flower of Fortune for Wyoming!

The city's splendors many a sylvan spot
Enfold, kept fresh and green for fair Wyo-
    ming;
The vale-queen's spell remains on grove and
    grot,
Though half their haunting legends are forgot;

While, by the river's bend, stands Summer, sum-
    ming
Thy varied, verdurous charms, flower-sweet
    Wyoming!

Over against the city's riotous shore
Majestic trees, nurslings of wild Wyoming,
Arise,—elm, maple, oak, and sycamore,—
Their domèd green delightful as of yore;
Harping the hymns sublime, or softly hum-
    ming
The lullabies they learned of wild Wyoming.

And what grand tales yon beauteous river
    tells,
A rhythmic flow, of far-away Wyoming!
And on the rustic legend how it dwells!
With winding panorama which impels
The wondering towns it turns to, in its roaming,
To weave still grander fables for Wyoming.

6

From the far glory of her girdling hills
To Flora's inmost fane, on fair Wyoming
Lingers a grace of outline fine, which fills
Brimful the sense of beauty! When morn spills
Its crystal rills, or sunset gold is foaming,
Once more the fays have found their fair Wyo-
     ming.

The Old romance, outdone, still finds her fair;
Half its romance the New owes fair Wyoming;
Her name forever! web and woof as rare
As erst enriched the legend-weaver's care!
First and last words of Wonder in the gloam-
     ing;
Her miniature immortal, fair Wyoming!

1888.

TO ERIN.

THIS sudden dark is but transition. Beautiful
    as Venus
  Beheld through Sorrow's sable glass, Hope
    hastes to Freedom's side,
Who cries to Erin through the cloud, "Bright
    shines the star between us;
  By very Hope am I eclipsed, the bridegroom
    by his bride!"

There is a light which breeds despair, whose
    blandest ray is blighting,
  The daylight of the desert born, that murders
    with its smile;
With golden quicksands pitiless the patient heart
    requiting,
  And here and there an oasis that blossoms to
    beguile.

There is a shadow, cast of Hope, which hides
   a living glory,
  When, like Queen Esther, for her race she
    dares the disk of day;
'Tis Love come closer to her Lord to tell her
   people's story,—
  Let Haman rear his scaffold high and Hatred
    have its way.

O Erin's Star, intensely bright, yet ever pure
   and tender,
  Familiar grown with Sorrow's face, as Sorrow
    hath with thine,
On Freedom's clouded brow falls full thy
   smile's unquenchèd splendor,
  Day hearkens to thee and adores! the dark-
    ness is divine!

   April 29, 1887.

OUR GOLDEN STAIRS.

Our babe had heard that pretty story,
　　With wonder in his eyes,
About the stairway, grand and golden,
　　High up the happy skies.

Four summers, for our boy, with flowers
　　Those golden stairs arrayed;
And four times all the stars of summer
　　Their steps with gold inlaid.

So often beauteous thoughts are uttered
　　By childhood unawares,
We half suspect our darlings traverse
　　In dreams those golden stairs.

One morn when ours was just awaking
　　Out of a gentle sleep,

A smile transfigured all his features,
  That held a meaning deep.

I said, my heart with bliss o'erflowing,
  That gloried in such cares,
"Come down with me," when quick he queried,
  "What! down the golden stairs?"

I pressed him to my heart so fondly,
  My heart sang out for joy;
And catching up the simple chorus,
  I sang it to my boy.

Methinks the stairs are golden,
  Because my boy in white
Comes down them every morning
  And up them every night.

Oh! did he fancy, on the summit
  Of rounded, rosy rest,

That dream-land out of which he wakened
  The Heaven of the Blest?

Or, waking, thought his splendid journey
  Was hardly finished yet;
And I, adown the steps remaining,
  Should carry him, my pet?

As well when childhood's happy visions,
  As those of older hearts,
Have floated off and left the real,
  The rapture soon departs.

When down its steps we both descended,
  And at the bottom stood,
Surprised, my child surveyed our stairway,
  And cried, "It's only wood!"

But soon, with childish, sweet persistence,
  When half a mind to scold,

He caught the sunlight on the varnish,
　And smiling said, "It's gold!"

Perhaps too young to deem it golden,
　For that his Heavenly Friend
And Father smiles upon his pathway,
　With Heaven at either end?

Again I clasped him, oh! so fondly,
　My heart sang out for joy;
When catching up the happy chorus,
　I sang it for my boy.

For this our stairs are golden,
　Our little angels bright
Come down them every morning,
　Go up them every night.

March 5, 1883.

THE LIGHTS THAT MOCK US.

THERE is no mockery in the smile of Morn,
  None in the dazzling Noonday's glance divine;
  The earnest Stars look down, with brows
    benign,
To bless the gentle dreams of Twilight born.
And e'en the merry Moon, a tinge of scorn
  That just escapes for mortal fancies fine,
  With all the mischief shadowed in her shine,
Smiles like a rose regretful of its thorn.

The lights of earth, which have a kindly glow
  And sweep of vision heavenly in its ken,
  Smile, in their seasons, on the sons of men,
Who meet the unfriendly shaft with bended bow.
  The gleams we follow vanish like the elves;
  The lights that mock us glimmer in our-
    selves.

COME IN MY DREAMS.

A SONG.

COME in my dreams and smile again,
   Come with the loving look of old;
This broken heart is happy then,
   And flutters free from sorrow's hold!
Come in my dreams and kiss again,
   The dear old fondness to renew—
I wake to find you false, but when
    I dream, oh! then so fond and true!

Come in my dreams, when slumber brings
   Forgetfulness of all my woe;
Come in sweet dreams, when fond Love wings
   The swallow flights of long ago,
And, from its home within the heart,
   Still cleaves the clouds that lie beyond;
And you shall nevermore depart,
   And I will nevermore despond!

Come in my waking hours no more,
　Unless it be with tearful eyes;
For close to sorrow's troubled shore
　Love, in a hopeless circle, flies,
And knows it ne'er can build again
　The broken nest from whence it flew—
I wake to find you false, but when
　I dream, oh! then so fond and true!

THE CYCLONE.

WHAT had Wyoming's hill-girt city
　To fear from her Cloudland fair?
Oft had our hearts been stirred with pity,
　But never yet with prayer,
With muttered curse and imprecation,
　From pallid lips outpoured,
When the fierce Wind-Fiends of Desolation
　Were unfettered by the Lord!
The Doom-Cloud's shadow was wont to en-
　　shroud
The homes of the West alone;
And what had our Valley, in shine or cloud,
　To fear from the far Cyclone?

Far different the picture on Nature's ken
　When the leonine storms from their lair up-
　　rose!

When, for man and beast, in meadow and glen,
And here, where the fair Susquehanna flows,
The strange unrest of a sultry day
To an unknown terror turned!
And the cinder-like sun in the glooming gray
Like a beacon of danger burned!

Never so dread was the black dome above us,
The clouds never wore so fierce a frown;
And even the Rain, that was still fain to love us,
Like the tears of the prophet, wept over the
town!

A crash through the clouds! 'Tis only the
thunder—
Ah! the tremors that follow its more distant peals!
While, before and behind, and over and
under,
Broods the horror that Nature already feels!

'Tis an outburst of rage from the fretting At-
    lantic !
  Nay, a home-brewed storm,—a hurricane
    waif !
Tall trees are toppled, the horses are frantic,
  Not a spot in the city that seems to be
    safe !

Not a doubter is left to make light of the
    danger ;
The oldest inhabitant daft as the stranger—
Behind houses, in hiding, crouch fear-stricken
    men,
Who fled from their shelter, and seek it again !
Hither and thither the bravest are speeding,
The fate of their friends and their neighbors
    unheeding !
No, no, 'tis for Love's sake the fugitives
    strive,—
The loved they may never again meet alive !

Sense of dread is not all in the hearing and
    seeing;
  The forebodings of woman are quickest to
    form—
Frightened wives, with their babes, to the cellar
    are fleeing,
  And some for their babes are braving the
    storm !
In the grasp of suspense, by great perils di-
    vided,
  The dear ones of home were never so dear;
But some, unaware of what has betided,
  The sweet lullaby sing, " There is nothing to
    fear !"

The Lightning's red finger the fire-bell tolls !
The smoke of the flame-fronted Tempest uprolls
From river to roadway, from roadway to
    street,—
Its flight up the valley less fatal than fleet,

And the trophies it tore from a neighboring
    vale

But as straws to the conquests in store for the
    gale.

Lo! deeper the gloom where opposing storms
    meet,

Both caught in the grip of a greater than they,

Defiant at first and now swift to obey,

But changing its course, while they hang on
    the verge,

And widen the sweep of its terrible scourge!

With the menace of death for a myriad of
    souls,

The smoke of the flame-fronted Tempest up-
    rolls

From the south of the city, eastwardly blown,—

" Fire !" the first outcry, and now " The Cy-
    clone !"

A moment ago men stood in its path

Who now scan its revels unscathed of its wrath !

"Thank God, we are saved!" the cry as it
veers.
It has swung to the right, and when it up-
rears,
Lo! the funnel-shaped cloud that every one
fears!

"A Cyclone!" "A Cyclone!" tells the tale
in a word:
Its shuddering sounds for miles may be
heard;
Its fierce hissing noises, its rumble and roar,
Are a hundredfold louder and terrify more
Than the rush of a runaway train in the
night,
In charge of a mad engineer,
Whose maniac shrieks and yells of delight
Were dreadful to hear,
As the engine, in agony, swept into sight;
Fear too affrighted to fear!

7*

And the crash that befell, when it came in
collision
 With another that dreamt not of danger
 ahead,
Was as naught to the wreck that is wrought,
in derision,
 By the awful Cyclone, with its dying and
 dead !

Rolling on in the dark of its own dread
creation,
 Black billows of smoke and half-smothered
 flame,
Like a monster, with headlights, that stops
at no station,
 It comes to destroy, and will go as it came !

Like the voice of the tempest, now low and
now high,
 Increasing in volume and terror of tone,

It rises and falls as it rolls through the sky,
  With forces unlooked for in league with
    its own !
And striking the ground, in its dance of de-
    struction,
  Spreads ruin more wide than its zigzag-
    ing path !
Drawing up to the maw of its maelstrom-
    like suction
  All the odds and the ends of its house-
    wrecking wrath !
The roof of a cottage that somebody cherished,
  The tree that had sheltered his shattered
    abode ;
Dread reminders of home and its inmates
    that perished,
  To heighten our fears and our horror to
    goad !
A cradle let fall where babe never crept,
  The shreds of a carpet that Beauty had trod ;

But, blind to its ridicule, man's humor
   slept;
  More fearful the scene because it was
   odd!

Steeds in full flight,—types of Fury Titanic,—
  The forecasts of Terror outdistanced by
   Death,
Or hurled, as they coursed o'er the pitfalls
   of panic,
  Into caverns that Ruin had built in a
   breath!

Prayer in a street-coach the storm-bombs
   were shelling;
  In a very simoom of thick-flying débris!
Wild shrieks of anguish in many a dwelling,—
  The warning too late from destruction to
   flee!

Dwellings, whose beauty had gladdened the
vision,
 In the tatters of ruin the strange tale to tell!
Solid structures it smote with appalling pre-
cision;
 Either razed to the ground or crushed like
a shell!

Mighty towers snapped off like the masts of a
vessel
 By this worse than a sea-storm, a-stalk o'er
the land;
And lo! where their Giants had gathered to
wrestle,
 What shipwrecks were strewn on Calamity's
strand!

Countless hearts with which it had cruelly toyed,
 Unstrung in the midst of the sorrow it
spread!
 f

Hundreds of homes in a twinkling destroyed,
And more than a score of the mangled and
dead !

The dirge has been sung, and the solemn bell
tolled,
Long ago for our loved, the young and the
old,
A score that were slain
By the dread Cyclone !
Let not its dirges be heard again,
For love's sake alone !
The tremble of bell, and of tear,
O'er the dust of our mangled dead,
Is forgot,—and forgotten, I fear,
When the shadows of terror had
fled,
The sincere and solemn thanksgiving
That was offered to God by the living.

Let us be grateful for evermore

That the graves we counted were only a
score !

'Tis the mad strength of Death and Destruction.

In a black, rushing cloud-rack confined,

That wrought into frenzy will brook no ob-
struction

From anything earthly, its kindred or kind;

From man, or his works, though he build
them of granite,

With the broadest foundations, the tallest of
towers ;

Like the Earthquake and Flood, the scourge
of our planet,

Lest men should grow vain in the pride of
their powers.

Not the thing of an hour! but casting aside

Its ebony chariot, whose courier is Fear,

From the region of air where mortals abide
  It ascends, it is said, to a loftier sphere;
Coursing the globe at a speed would erase
Every vestige of life and of love from its face!
But the circuits of Terror it sweeps not alone:
Its number is thousands, its name, The Cy-
    clone!

To planes far above us in mercy uplifted,
  Narrow its path and eccentric its flight;
And mortals give thanks when its movements
    are shifted
  From the hamlets and cities it fills with
    affright!

1891.

IRELAND AND HER MARTYRS.

I.

Voices of eloquence and poesy
  And song, poured on the breeze by deathless
    lips,
That lead the universal symphony
  Of freedom; you would suffer no eclipse
If, pausing now in mid-flight of your theme,
  You caught the plaintive note of yon sad
    Land,
In whose torn breast freedom is but a dream,
  And baffled hope an inward burning brand!
Forgetful of the feuds of race or clan,
  Undaunted by the clash of differing creeds,
Remembering alone man's debt to man,
  And all the world is kin in direst needs,
Should follow then so grand a Marseillaise,
Tyranny would turn and flee the enchanted
    place!

II.

The birthday of a patriot martyr slain
  For love of liberty, where men are free,
  Is fitting time for joy and jubilee;
But such a day is pierced with thrilling pain,
E'en though the glory of his death remain,
  If for his land it brought not liberty,
  Or some sure sign its dawning soon would be
Hope's heralding he had not died in vain!
  The death-days of thy heroes, Land of ours,
When all the sudden overflow of tears
  Hath ebbed away, grow fragrant with sweet
      flowers;
And for the "sobbing bells" the nation hears
  The shrilly clarions of a glowing morn
  The day repeat when Liberty was born.

III.

But thou, sad Isle!—forever fresh and green
  In the fond memory of thy children here,

Though thy sweet grasses withered were and
    sere,—
How many mournful deaths thy soil hath seen!
With naught but growing sorrows spread be-
    tween;
    And following hard upon the martyr's bier
    The footsteps of fell woe, and want, and fear;—
O Sorrow's Isle! how hard thy lot hath been!
    And for thy suffering heroes what harsh doom,
That did not grant thee what they died to
    gain!
    In all this wide, wide world a little room,
A little space for them who would remain
    To live and die like freemen—simple boon—
    Beneath their own bright skies and harvest
    moon!

IV.

Yet something in brave Emmet's breast was
    fain
    To picture Ireland free! the hero heard

Afar his rescued country's happy strain,

    And read her unwrit history word by word.

He felt that his young life was a sweet leaven

    Ireland's after-times should so pervade,

She still would find the favoring smile of

        Heaven,

    Though in the dust his loving heart was laid;

And from the night that wrapped his dust in

        gloom

    A clear, unclouded dawn would some time rise,

And his dear, dead country come forth of the tomb

    Of Tyranny, with the day-spring in her eyes;

While friendly lands should scatter at her feet

Freedom's fair flowers, that smell so fresh and

        sweet!

V.

O Isle of many griefs! henceforth take heart,

    The still, small voice in England's yielding

        breast,

Till you are free, will never give her rest—

England herself at last will say, " Depart
In peace."   For ah! not always by the art
  Of statesmanship or arms may Empire wrest
  A people's God-given rights away; the test
Is truth divine, from brute force far apart!
  Erin, take heart! the day is not far off;
For friend and foe alike do force the time;
    God never heeds man's favor or his frown.
  Though pride of power resist, and hatred scoff,
The omens of the century are sublime—
    The love of right grows stronger than the
    Crown.

1880.

8*

DESERTING THE FLAG OF THE STARRY EYES.

In the glorified cavalry garb of the Union
   A shadow, like mine, but in mien too brave
With a soldier that faltered to hold communion,
   Comes hinting to me of a flower-strewn grave,
Of his ghostly rides in the ranks of glory,
   And my part in the patriot's paradise!
'Tis a dream of his; the deserter's story
   Is known to the Flag of the Starry Eyes!

More in fear of the flag than the ban I was
     under,
   When I fled in the charge that was lance to
     lance;
I heard her voice in the cannon's thunder,
   And my heart seemed to shrivel beneath her
     glance

Where the battle raged; but alas! I dallied
  With the moment when manhood lives or
    dies;
And when my courage had fairly rallied,
  I fled from the scorn of her beautiful eyes!

At every turn she uprose before me,
  On the battle-cloud with its lightning flame;
And the spell of her grandeur in action came
    o'er me,
  With Freedom beside her, and deathless
    Fame!
But still I fled, for the step had been taken;
  Then a shout of victory shook the skies,
And lo! it was I who had been forsaken,
  Not the charioted queen of the starry eyes!

My battle-scars for naught had counted,
  Were they shown to her in her fierce dis-
    dain;

With the sabre-stroke, on my charger mounted,
  I might seek for her dear old smile in vain!
So I spurred my horse, in my mad despairing,
  Tow'rd the shallows of shame, to his great
    surprise;
And I felt that a hero my shame was sharing,—
  With his head thrown back tow'rd her
    beckoning eyes!

But he wheeled about, with the wildest neigh-
    ing,
  His love for her trumpeting far and wide,
With the sweep of a whirlwind her gesture
    obeying,
  As he plunged into victory's swelling tide.
She patted his neck as in approbation,—
  My Nemesis now in a charger's guise,—
While the touch of her filled me with conster-
    nation,
  And a cowering dread of her flashing eyes!

Thenceforward he ran bereft of a rider,
    With my blood as a balm for his wounded pride;
And the gulf between us grew darker and wider,
    Till it moaned like the sea when its storms
        subside.
But the scorn of the Flag there was no escaping:
    Wherever I went she was sure to rise,
Unfurled to the sight or of fancy's own shaping,
    With the torments of hell in her soul-haunt-
        ing eyes!

I wandered away in a trance of terror,
    Away from the Flag, and the faces of men!
And my farther flight was a fatal error,
    For the refuge sought I have failed to gain.
But oh! if I knew in my isolation
    That they mourn me for dead and my memory
        prize,
I would crave of death's angel emancipation
    From the maddening thrall of her myriad eyes!

I have grayed since then less with years than
    sorrow,
  On this shore more lonely than ocean-isle;
But perchance I shall sight a sail to-morrow,
  And catch from afar her forgiving smile!
The winds and the waves will attest my con-
    trition,
  She has smiled in my dreams and heard all
    my sighs,
And never had soldier a heavenlier vision
  Who has walked with Despair, 'neath her still,
    starry eyes!

I plead not the laurels I wore when I faltered,
  Nor the fever-racked frame to the battle I
    brought,
But the love which the hardship of fate has not
    altered,
  And a heart that beats true in a bosom dis-
    traught.

Oh! the touch of her folds! how it thrilled
    through and through me
  When she smiled in my dreams and gave ear
    to my sighs!
But waking, I fear that her glance would undo me,
  Bending over me so with her beautiful eyes!

Lo! a friendly sail! the banner flying
  That embraces the world in her peaceful
    dream!
While prone on the strand is a soldier dying
  Of a broken heart and her starry gleam!
Let his name be dropped from the roll-call of
    glory
  And classed with deserters, but do not despise;
For the love of the Flag is an unfinished
    story
  Without the forgiveness that falls from her
    eyes!

1889.

SAINTED AT SEVEN.

SWEET sunshine plays around my dwelling,
  And pleasures hive their precious store;
O tearless heart! there is no telling
  What sorrows wait without thy door.

Mother, press closer to your bosom
  The child you lately feared to lose;
For every household has its blossom,
  And Death stands doubting which to choose.

Thick gloom enfolds my neighbor's dwelling,
  A lovely child of seven lies dead;
But oh! through sorrow's sudden knelling
  Her sweet voice falls: "Be comforted."

One sweet tone threads the solemn tolling:
  "Beloved of all, and only seven;"
96

While, from above, still more consoling:
"Seven means safe with Christ in heaven."

Enter, dear Christ, grief's darkened dwelling,
And comfort them who weep to-night;
And with thy presence, peace-compelling,
Fill all the house with heavenly light.

THE HUNDRED AND FORTY-THIRD.

(A TYPICAL REGIMENT.)

Written for and read at the Reunion of the One Hundred and Forty-Third Regiment P. V., at Camp Luzerne, August 26, 1891.

ON our far-famed Valley what glory falls
   Like the deeds of The Hundred and Forty-
      Third?
The service to Freedom their story recalls,
   On our beautiful Valley the crown they con-
      ferred!
The men who remembered the Patriot's tomb
   And the dust of the martyrs in Liberty's
      urn!
What splendor uplighted the fair Valley's
      gloom
   Like that which was kindled in Camp Lu-
      zerne?

98

A band of the boldest from hill-side and glen,

The ready-made heroes of forest and mine,

Our foremost and first, all brave-hearted men!

And Liberty smiled when they fell into line

And followed her lead, eleven hundred strong,

The Flag of the Free, and the Sword of
the Brave,

To the fife and the drum that enchanted the
throng,

When they marched to the front the Union
to save.

Devoted to duty in camp-life and drill,

Upbuilding a fort, or marching through mire,

Supporting an army at Chancellorsville

As if they had not been but once under
fire!

In the swamp and corn-stubble as ready to
serve

The colors they bore as in battle array;

From none of war's hardships willing to swerve,
The Flag's firm defenders forever and aye!

With a leader who loved them far more than
his life,
With a love that outweighed all the laurels
of war,
And officered so for the terrible strife,
Not a corporal there that you could not adore,
Not a private of whom you would not be proud;
And the zeal on their features was some-
thing divine,
As they chafed to come under the black battle-
cloud,
That the sunshine of Freedom the sooner
might shine.

Oh! these were the heroes, and men of like
mould,
With the Keystone itself in Confederate reach,

The fearless invader in firm check to hold,
　To lead the attack, or fill up the breach;
To fight three to one, and change front under fire,
　And fight on, unsupported, while others re-
　　treat;
Fire volley on volley, when forced to retire,
　While the rebel flood-tide rolled up at their feet!

Ay, these and their comrades, now Dana's
　　brigade,
　Who had charged and destroyed three bri-
　　gades in the fray,
Deserve deathless fame for the firm stand they
　　made,
　When they kept a whole army for five hours
　　at bay!
The key of the first day's defence in their
　　keeping,
　"We have come here to stay," the cry first
　　and last;

9*

And there to this day are some of them sleep-
     ing,
  Where the bugle recalls their brave battle-
     blast.

Ah! well may we look for a valor like theirs
  To find its full flower in that living ro-
     mance,
When their brave color-sergeant a whole army
     dares,
  With clinched fist defying its sweeping ad-
     vance.
Their Nemesis incarnate was facing them then,
  A finger prophetic, his finger of scorn!
For Crippen had caught, on his clear, dying ken,
  The first flush of the triumph to come with
     the morn!

" Rally on your colors!" Conyngham cried,
  "Rally, One Hundred and Forty-Third!"

" Rally on your colors!" DeLacy replied,

  And the action was suited then and there

    to the word;

And all the boys rallied, the colors were saved,

  Crippen himself by his comrades outdone!

Ever thus have the soldiers of Freedom behaved;

  In this way the war for the Union was won.

When the dread morning broke on the third

    day's fight,

  With artillery havoc unheard of before,

And Lee's legions at last came surging in

    sight,

  They still did their duty in Doubleday's corps!

The artillery's target, supporting the left,

  As if rebel revenge marked them out for its

    prey,

Springing up in the path its avalanche cleft,

  'Gainst Wilcox and Pickett helped carry the

    day.

Superhuman your valor, ye brave volunteers,
   In your State and your hearth-stones' immor-
      . tal defence;
So heightening the zeal of your gallant com-
      peers,
   All the homes of the free seemed in breath-
      less suspense.
So the North's brave battalions fought on, to a
      man,
   As if each its own firesides were struggling
      to save;
" For the land of the free," the fierce battle began,
   But the fight's loud refrain was " The home
      of the brave !"

With scarcely a thought of the glory they won,
   The country in peril their uppermost care,
Still it lightened their hearts, the knapsack and
      gun,
   The burdens of march and manœuvre to bear.

Always true to their trust, wherever they stood,
  The Capitol guarding, or goading the foe;
Whether merry or sad was the veterans' mood,
  The stern voice of Duty they ne'er failed
    to know.

Right well had they earned the camp's wel-
    come rest,
  Recruiting their ranks and their own crip-
    pled powers;
But the day had not dawned of their uttermost
    test,
  Though its shadow lay dark on the long
    winter hours!
And its shadow is flung on the glories of
    May,
  And the Rapidan runs like a river of tears;
'Tis night in the Wilderness while yet it is day,
  For Doomsday has burst on our brave vol-
    unteers!

Like wild beasts in the woods the batteries roar
  Like Gehenna the smoke of the conflict as-
    cends,
As it withers the flower of the First Army
    Corps,
  On whose blindfolded bravery the battle
    depends.
Here were horrors to war hitherto unknown,
  When Glory to Agony yielded the crown!
The battle-shout here was a shuddering groan,
  And Triumph itself wore a grim, ghastly
    frown!

Like courage incarnate these foemen had met,
  And the butchery lasted day after day;
Compassion was dead, not an eyelid was wet,
  For the fury of hell had laid hold of the fray;
So fierce it relentlessly followed the dead,
  To the brows of the dying the death-damp
    denied;

For the fires of the brush were the shrouds
that it spread,
The charred trees the sole mourners that
wailed at their side.

But the undaunted heroes of Dana's brigade,—
Who, wounded and captured, could lead them
no more,—
When Mercer was killed, fought on undis-
mayed,
With their dying behind them and duty before!
When wounded still fought, and laughed at
their wounds;
Fought on till they died—it was fitting they
should—
Against foemen whose courage acknowledged
no bounds,
In that caldron of battle and brave men's
blood!

In the boldest relief 'gainst that background of
　　gloom
　Was the improvised fight of the Second
　　Brigade,
When Glory her lost smile was seen to re-
　　sume
　At the wild charge its men under Conyng-
　　ham made!
Detached from your friends, in what savored of
　　rout,
　You must needs keep on fighting, and rallied
　　again
On finding the colors that Osborne hung
　　out
　At the famous Cross Roads for his own fear-
　　less men!

Retaking the battery that Hancock had lost,
　In the face of its guns and a hand-to-hand
　　fight—

Heaven knows why you came there, when sore
    battle-tossed,
  If 'twas not to help Hancock put Longstreet
    to flight!
Hancock driven back with his troops in re-
    treat,
  Major Osborne rode up and gave the com-
    mand,
And you soon laid the prize at the General's feet,
  With your five or six hundred, a brave-
    hearted band!

Your regiment's dread decimation attests
  The proud part that you took in those terri-
    ble days,
And with lustre more lasting your valor in-
    vests
  Than anything else that is said in its praise.
The morning reports that its companies kept
  Had pathos to touch e'en a veteran's soul;

In the sound of the bugle a slight tremor
  crept,
  While a pitiful remnant answered the roll!

Eighty strong to the fight each company came,
  But it tugs at the heart-strings the remnants
    to see,
As one scans the reports—the rest average the
    same—
  Of the nine, twelve, and eighteen of A, K,
    and G!
Dead and living their heroes too many to name,
  Though the regiment adds to the army's re-
    nown;
Commanders and men all deserving of fame,
  Without naming the patriots, we point to their
    crown.

But the Union's vast sacrificial fount,
  With its rivers of blood, must still higher rise;

With many a grim mile-stone of battle to count
  On the steep, gory path that ahead of you
    lies.
Cold Harbor to come, with its hopeless as-
    sault,
  Its glory and slaughter, the grimmest of these
But a star still beckons from Victory's vault;
  To the gates of Success Grant still holds the
    keys.

In the siege and assault, when the river is crossed,
  A share of its grandeur your regiment
    claims;
The Confederate Malakoff hopelessly lost,
  The jasper of glory thrown back on the
    James!
From summit to summit of splendor you
    march,
  Every fight that you wage is fought in its
    shine;

The rainbow of Hope spans the North's
  clouded arch,
  But the work done beneath it is still more
  divine.

From your cold winter-quarters, still seen in
  your dreams,
  You catch its bright rays with the opening
  of spring,
And they blend, as you fight, with your bayo-
  net gleams,
  As o'er Hatcher's Run their halo they fling.
" Charging the fortifications" your last
  Fitting work, and how glorious the word—
Duty the first and last mile-stone you passed—
  For men like The Hundred and Forty-Third!

On our far-famed Valley what glory falls
  Like the deeds of The Hundred and Forty-
  Third?

No sweet sounds more sad than its faint bugle-
calls,

None more brave when in war-time their
echoes were heard;

None sadder. Your dear old Commander is
dead,

At rest with the heroes of whom he was
fond;

But the glow of their smiles on your camp-fire
is shed,

And sweet is the bugle that calls from beyond!

August 22–25, 1891.

h 10*

SHERIDAN.

As rain-laden roses droop low on the stem,

So droopeth to-day Columbia's fair Gem

'Neath a cloud-burst of grief! The Flag at
half-mast,

With heart-breaking news from Nonquitt at
last!

All suddenly shrouded in sorrow, the while

'Twas trembling with rapture 'neath Sheridan's
smile!

Like the wife of his bosom kneeling down when
he died,

And the comforting angels who knelt at her
side,

So the Flag of his Country bends low over him,

With a pride in its bosom that tears cannot
dim,

114

That swells its bright folds till they glisten and
    gleam
Like the fond smile of love in a sorrowful
    dream!
Like a dream seems his death,—and so cruel
    the while
The sunshine of hope came with Sheridan's
    smile.

O Banner beloved! in the depths of thy blue
Glassing deeds that are golden forever anew;
The god in his look, whose likeness they
    caught
In the one supreme moment with destiny
    fraught,
In the crisis of battle, the crash and the
    strain,
Unmatched in thy memory shall ever remain!
Unveil as of yore, our grief to beguile,
The sunburst of triumph in Sheridan's smile.

Like Columbia, the beautiful Queen of the Free,
The Flag bows in sorrow on land and on
      sea,
And sobs for a soldier as true and as brave
As a land ever loved or God ever gave;
Its stars all in tears, and its stripes all aflame,
While it wreathes this memorial round Sheri-
      dan's name:
"No gem decks the Crown of the Union re-
      stored
Like the gleam of the glory of Sheridan's
      sword."

Admired of the world, by the army adored,
Let the tears of his comrades bejewel his
      sword;
In the sheath of white roses that Peace has en-
      twined
Be the blade that is blameless forever en
      shrined!

Touch gently, kind winds, the draped Banner
    that weeps,—
In the love of its bosom the worn hero sleeps,—
Till it findeth, enfolding a heart without guile,
Death's shadows have vanished in Sheridan's
    smile.

August 8, 1888.

THE LAST OF THE THREE.

LISTEN, Atlanta!
  Be still, O sorrowing sea!
A bugle-note, sad yet consoling,
Kindling our pride and our grief controlling,
  Is blown of the lips of Glory,
    On the camping-ground of the Free,
For the last of our three great Captains,
  The last of the Three!

Meed of his triumphs from Chattanooga
  Down to Atlanta, his march divine,
Revealed in the genius akin to mercy
  A bulwark stronger than battle-line!

In his last lonely march victorious,
  Lo! on the shadowy shore,
118

Sherman, with Grant and Sheridan,
And the last of our three great Admirals,
  Who sailed a day before!

From the farthest north to Atlanta,
  From Atlanta to the sea,
The tolling bells, still a-tremble
For the last of the naval trio
  That sailed on the silent sea,
Give voice to the people's affection
For the soldier who loses no lustre,
  When we think, with a thrill, of the Three!

In the sweet peace they conquered together,
In Liberty's own golden weather,
  Let all the bells tearfully tremble
    The loving farewells of the Free,
For the last of our great Commanders,
    The last of Three!

February 19, 1891.

WHEN DEATH HAD LOST THE DAY.

WHILE yet she trod the rosy ways

    Of childhood, pure and sweet,

She met the Master's tender gaze,

    And worshipped at His feet;

And thus from infant innocence

    To conscious faith she passed,

And steadfast proved till she went hence

    To be with Him at last;

Her path to Joy's celestial sphere

    Victorious all the way,

There was no time in her career

    When Death could win the day.

Had Death surprised her in her glee

    O'er childhood's gathered flowers,

'Twere fraught with less felicity
   Than were her dying hours,
When, garlanded by angels fair
   With heaven's immortal bloom,
She smiled amidst our mute despair,
   "Triumphant o'er the tomb,"
And sang her Saviour led the way
   To heaven's perennial bowers—
'Twas meet, since Death had lost the day,
   To deck the dead with flowers!

From the sweet age of twelve, and up
   Through woman's fewer years,—
O sorrowing hearts! the bitter cup
   Is brimmed with happy tears,—
There was such sunshine in her eyes,
   Such sweetness in her smile,
Her spirit back from Paradise
   The earth could not beguile.

The perfect life she has attained,

'Mid fields that bloom alway,

And knows more fully what she gained

When Death had lost the day!

May, 1889.

THE ROSES OF RAPTURE AND REST.

WHITE rose, arrayed for joy or sorrow,
    Friend of the living and dead,
While from terrestrial founts you borrow
    The fragrance you calmly shed,—
Love's tale of bliss and grief's sad story
    Telling in the very same breath,—
To invisible skies you owe the glory
    That links you to life and death!

Red rose, full many a storm outlasting,
    A zephyr shall lay you low;
Then all in vain about you casting
    For the friends you used to know!
The flattering touch of soft white fingers
    And Beauty's enchanting smile—

The twilight of love that around you lingers—
  You shall lose in a little while.

For the happier lot of the white rose sighing,
  To press dead Beauty's cheek,
To follow the dead and comfort the dying—
  'Tis rest for yourself you seek,
Red rose, consumed by a passionate longing
  For the bliss that is only a dream;
With the dreams you awaken, too often wronging
  The dwellers by Life's fair stream.

The lore of death from the white rose learning,
  Life's mystery yours, red rose;
The fires of love in your bosom burning,
  Breath of rapture, but not repose.
The white rose is Beauty's diviner reflection,
  Where every hue plays its part;
And purity is but the sweet perfection
  Of harmony in the heart.

Red rose, you have shared in the triumphs of
    Beauty,
  But the white is her dying choice;
The flower that hallowed the paths of duty,
  And shared in her sinless joys!
Red roses for him who died for glory,
  Or, better, who battled for Right!
But when we have heard their heroic story,
  The roses that rest him are white.

11*

THE BEAUTIFUL DEAD.

Lines on the death of the deeply-lamented Harrison Wright, Ph.D.,
a Wyoming Valley historian and poet of great promise.

THE souls that were brave, and whose footsteps
    were dutiful,
  And love was the light they shed,
Whose deeds made their lives, when living, beau-
    tiful,
  Surely these are the Beautiful Dead.

And lo! 'mong the noble of memory's number-
    ing,
  Some lives so surpassing fair,
Like the roses that bloom while the dead are
    slumbering,
  Their beauty forbids despair.

126

Of such was the friend of the choosing and
cherishing,
Alike of the young and the old,—
Friendship, sweet in the leaf, as after the perish-
ing,
And at heart as fragrant to hold.

Oh! flower of filial love's fondest engendering,
Fearless glance of immortal, kind eyes!
Oh! smile of the brave, all self-love surrendering!
Kind voice! the heart's pleasant surprise.

Kind eyes! and yet keen, that turned so for-
bearingly
From the bad to the good in a friend;
Rare, gifted intelligence! smiting not sparingly
The wares the false teacher would vend.

He loitered not where the lotus was flowering,
And fled from the blight of its bloom;

But he loved the bright dreams of Nature's own
    dowering,
  A stranger to grief and to gloom.

For him all beauty was ever in blossoming,
  His mind was a garden in bloom!
And Science, to him her secrets unbosoming,
  Were legend most meet for his tomb.

His tireless quest, the honey of history,
  For winters ahead had hived;
And of fading traditions—despite Death's mys-
    tery,
  Say not he was short-lived.

A light indistinct Death's deeps are borrowing,—
  'Tis the Dawn, with its deathless rays;
Yet we weep, and for soul so lovable sorrowing,
  Every tear is a pearl of praise.

The heart that was brave, and whose friendship
    was beautiful,
  The spirit such lustre that shed,
Now reaps the reward of the wise and the
    dutiful
  In the home of the Beautiful Dead.

MY PRETTY BOY.

My pretty boy!—'tis love, not praise, that speaks;
Fond words grow flower-gay in the light of
    joy,—
By more than sparkling eyes and shapely
    cheeks,
        My pretty boy!

Puck's hands, with sleepy hollows for each toy,
Small mouth melodious when the kiss it seeks,
The smile distorting grief cannot destroy;

A straggling tear compassion quickly piques,
Pouting with sweet cries clogged that never
    cloy,
Your thoughts are butterflies, your footprints
    freaks,
        My pretty boy!

HIS FIRST FIRE-CRACKER.

'Twas his first fire-cracker that pointed the way
   To patriotism, and taught him to take
A personal part in the glorious day,
    When we want all the music that powder
      can make.

In its faint hissing sound he fancied he heard
   The stir of the storm on the tyrant that
    fell;
On its fire-kindling tongue the first whispered
    word
   That found louder utterance in Liberty's
    Bell.

No bird-note so thrilling, no rose-bud so fair,
   As that red-coated minstrel of freedom and
    right

That sang in his hand and hurrahed in the
    air,
That fell like a soldier and died of delight.

The first streak of Liberty's dawn he descried
    In its slow-kindling spark and its sunburst
        at last;
The rout of the red-coats and all it implied,
    The carnage and smoke where its fragments
        were cast.

The crackers he fired are the spokes of the
        wheels
    That bring Freedom's chariot partly to view;
And their sparks are the stars that the rocket
        reveals,
    With a rush, when it flings out the red,
        white, and blue.

Now his patriotism needs pack upon pack,
With their musketry music and drum-rolls
of joy;
Every Fourth a step forward on glory's steep
track,
If he shows half the spunk that he had
when a boy.

December 21, 1889.

12

WHAT AILS THE GAEL?

WHAT ails the Gael, and all his kin,
  The wide world o'er?
Though bright his smile has always been,
  'Tis brighter than before.
Quoth he, and all his Celtic kin,
  " 'Tis brighter than before."

What has his laughter glorified?
  What is't he sees?
The ripple of the turning tide,
  The music of the breeze!
Quoth he, and every Celt beside,
  " The ripple and the breeze."

How calm he looks! What is't he hears?
  The angry seas?

Nay, while the sky above him clears,
  The ripple and the breeze!
Quoth they, while Freedom's visage clears,
  "The ripple and the breeze."

Behold! on every shore he stands,
  With victory's mien;
He and his cousins clasping hands,
  With smile serene.
Quoth they, "And Freedom understands
  That smile serene."

Though 'gainst the century's setting sun
  Dark racks arise,
Lo! how the smiling ripples run
  From countless Celtic eyes!
"Nay, nay, 'tis Freedom's rising sun,"
  The ready Celt replies.

What ails the Gael, and all his kin,
 The wide world o'er?
Though bright his smile has always been,
 'Tis brighter than before.
Quoth he, and all his Celtic kin,
 " 'Tis brighter than before."

LAUGHTER AND TEARS.

One smile begets another,
   The long face hides a laugh;
If half our smiles are happy,
   Why not the other half?

How oft our tears are tempted,
   In rolling down, to laugh!
If half our tears are happy,
   Why not the other half?

Speak, glad, salt tears hilarious,
   That drench the hearty laugh!
If half the heart be happy,
   Why not the other half?

When smiles and tears are wedded
   Is born the brightest laugh;

And then the tear is truer
And tenderer, too, by half.

So let them be united,
Lone tear and widowed laugh;
And who shall say that laughter
Is not the better half?

1886.

"REDDY," THE RIVER HERO.

(Charles Shannon, for whose life-saving services on the Delaware River the Philadelphia *Press* raised a fund by public subscription.)

WHEN "Where's my hat?" in "Reddy's" ear
　　Some rescued rascal shouted,
"The pitying angel" of the pier
　　His duty never doubted.
'Tis clear, who clamors for his hat
　　To life is closer clinging,
And "Reddy's" merry smile thereat
　　Has set life's river singing:
"O river death, down Delaware,
　　Though darkly deep embedded,
Thy crying waifs, in 'Reddy's' care,
　　Come back to me bareheaded!"

When "Where's my cap?" with saucy mien,
　　Demands a well-doused urchin,

On " Reddy's" face a smile is seen,
  Some inward comfort searchin'.
Though laughing-glad he picked him up,
  The while death's teeth did water,
For those who spurn life's sparkling cup
  He makes it hot and hotter;
Yet one mute grief his big heart rocks,—
  His boy! that drowned, without him,
The little darling of the docks,
  With such bright ways about him!

Through many a year he guarded well
  Those downward-wending by-ways,
And helped them find, who hapless fell,
  Life's fairer-looming highways.
Hope's grimy angel! white within
  As a happy seraph's pinions,
That moves athwart the paths of sin,
  And leads to life's dominions!

Whose honored head of golden hair,
  Amid the darkness glowing,
A tender star, down Delaware,
  Dips where 'tis deathward flowing!

Since all beheld his modest blush,
  He's more than ever "Reddy,"
And though he feel a little flush,
  He'll ne'er turn out unsteady.
Because he has an angel's heart,
  Let wealth's love-lifted pinions
Now give his faithful feet a start
  Towards pleasure's bright dominions!
And yet, just as of old, he'll jump
  Into the jaws of danger,
While in his throat's a choking lump
  For many a little stranger.

Place, too, the medal on his breast,
  Where sorrow finds a brother;

The badge of golden deeds confest
   Shall far outshine the other!
Some, wrought when boyhood's playful pranks
   Announced him on the river;
But not one word of simple thanks
   Did they—the saved—deliver!
And still he's young,—for him in store
   What glory unrecorded,
Who thought, if he might rescue more,
   He were full well rewarded!

August 22, 1884.

THE PENNY.

WHEN Mammon, in a merry mood,
First pleads to doubting babyhood
    The beauty of the penny,
Love plays a laughing interlude
    With captive kisses many.
And when it falls from baby's hands,
Time turns his glass of glittering sands
    For baby's sake, if any,
    While penny follows after penny!

Is it the coin's too sordid touch
Relaxes baby's gleeful clutch
    Or jolly-jointed jumble?
The thought amuses Mammon much,
    When it should make him humble;
Love thinks she hears her darling say
(And if he follow in that way

His feet will never stumble),
"Kiss me, and let the penny tumble."

When Mammon grave, in mercy's guise,
Stoops down where some starved infant lies
    To dole the dusky penny,
Time hides the tear-drops in his eyes,
    And Mammon hasn't any;
Fond Love is dead; no merry kiss,
Nor playful penny gone amiss,
    And never one too many—
    There's somehow pathos in a penny.

To such as these Time's busy hands
Show not his smiling, singing sands,
    Save only to embolden.
With them for bread the penny stands,
    And not for pastime golden.

Oft trembling on starvation's brink,

Time's golden grains sing sad, they think,

    Their hearts too early olden,

      And griefless death grows strangely

      golden!

1883.

SALT-WATER SONG.

THE sea is a city of shifting streets
   And constantly crumbling walls,
And the dwellers therein are lithe athletes
   That laugh when a structure falls,
With "a windy day," when its tottering towers
   Come tumbling about their ears—
When their houses are shattered they say, " It
     showers,"
   And, levelled at length, " It clears."

They halloo loud to Luna, 'tis all in her eye
   That she squanders her silver and gold
To build on their lots, while she lives in the
     sky,
   But when would a woman be told?
They mock at the lady, and feigning to pout
   At the rocking roofs she rears,

" Now hadn't she better put us all out,
　　Or gather the rents in arrears."

Then, shaking with laughter, exhort her to try
　　Not to get full any more.
When the rollicking winds come sweeping by
　　And swallow the roofs with a roar,
They ask how her man is, and why she looks
　　　　wan,
　　Is she coming to make repairs,
And why don't the lady, if she has a man,
　　Let him manage her vast affairs.

Then the storm's golden trumpets strike up a
　　　　tune
　　And the nimble athletes a dance;
And they ask him to join them,—the " Man "
　　　　of the Moon,—
　　Who is ready to jump at the chance !

'Mid melody soft as the voice of a dove,
    And music would shatter our ears,
They waltz on the waves, and, falling in love,
    Dip down in it deep with their dears.

The sea is a country vast and wild,
    With mountains that melt in mist,
And valleys where never a flower has smiled,
    Except in a mermaid's fist;
But the dwellers therein are always cool,
    In country and city the same;
And if fretful man is a sweltering fool,
    He has none but himself to blame.

THE JUDGE AND THE REF-
EREE.

(A COMEDY OF CARELESS PUNCTUATION.)

THEY made me a referee
    In a land case uncommon long-winded,—
An ill wind that blew a good fee,
    Because for a *fee* they contended.

And I said to myself my report
    Is lucid, at least to my own mind,
And when it goes up to the Court
    On the usual exceptions, though stone-blind,

Dame Justice will see what I mean—
    But wit, too, is blinding by flashes,
And a stroke of it might intervene,
    Should she lay the law down on my dashes.

And behold! from my findings of fact
  The Judge found—when he looked at my
      dashes—
The plaintiff possessed of the tract,
  And then follows his wit, with its flashes.

" Possessed of the piece in dispute
  (What more could a plaintiff desire ?)
At the time that he started the suit,
  And upwards of forty years prior !"

Did it take me ten days to find out,
  With a cursory sort of digression,
What the whole impish case was about,
  And who was in *peaceful* possession ?

There were acres one hundred and three,—
  Perchance more altogether were aching
To get a small slice of that fee,—
  And the title to three it was *taking.*

The plaintiff one hundred *possessed!*
   But his *deeds* called for three in addition!—
He ought to be sorely distressed,
   But, dear Judge, I don't mean in *perdition.*

I said what I meant, and I meant
   What I said, and I say that I said it!
It is not what I *wrote* I repent,
   But the cursory way that you *read* it.

The defendant's attorney, he took
   Two days my dull mind to enlighten—
Oh! the fists, in my face, that he shook
   To inform me, you see, not to frighten.

Now he claims my report is sent back
   That the case may again be *gone over!*
How the sides of old Laughter will crack
   When that bull gets again in the clover!

But I think I can stand the attack—
　At ten dollars a day till it's ended;
To go up again and come back
　On a teeter like that is just splendid!

How fine to ascend and descend
　On that seesaw aforesaid astraddle!
With law points, to boot, at each end,
　And myself, as it were, in the saddle.

THE DEMAND FOR MR. DEPEW.

(Expected guest of the Wilkesbarre *Eisteddfod*.)

Sons of Saint Patrick, hinder not his flight,
Though laughter languish at your banquet-board;
His heart with every race in kind accord,
His life a candle set on Freedom's height,—
Love's hands must needs have lit so kind a light,
For the oppressed its brightest rays out-
        poured,—
The Welsh, your Celtic cousins, have implored
Your frequent guest for just one glorious night.

Let no man hinder him, nor time nor tide—
He comes to hear a thousand nightingales,
Singing as sweet as in their native Wales,
Till, tasting heaven, his heart be satisfied;
But what a hush among those matchless birds
At Chauncey's silvery voice and golden words!

March 9, 1892.

"LETHE, AND OTHER POEMS,
1 8 8 2."

(Lines written on the fly-leaf of a copy presented to the editor of the Boston *Pilot* in 1884.)

WITH a long face I clung to this lachrymose
maiden,

    Till we met in a mirth-making mirror,—not
after;

Since she wouldn't be happy at all without
Aiden,

    I have cast, in seclusion, my life-lot with
Laughter.

If the ghost of her here out of Lethe affright
you,

The end that she came to will doubtless delight you.

154

Some said here is trash, some called her a
   treasure,
  But a faintness afflicted the praises that fol-
    lowed;
She died, but had left me, I noted with pleas-
   ure,
  "The dust" on the shelf for the taffy I
    swallowed.
I've a likeness or two left out of ten hun-
   dred,
But why I had any all the wags wondered.

One review that I read was a dismal death-
   notice,
  To an epitaph turning my dull dedica-
    tion;
The beam in his eye that knows well where a
   mote is
  The critic consumed in her instant crema-
    tion,

And would sink in the Lethe he mortally
    dreaded
Me, the maiden, and all, for he snatched me
    bald-headed.

But why send her picture to John Boyle
    O'Reilly,
  Who knows not, perhaps, that she ever
    existed?
" Why not?" says my second love, whispering slyly,
  " The smiles of O'Reilly cannot be resisted,
For they straighten wry faces and broad ones
    make brighter"—
Here she goes, though his smiles should like
    scimitars smite her.

For the first time we met when he came here
    canoeing,
  One moment with many admiring friends
    sharing,

When I felt in his glance were a dullard's un-
doing,

  With a kind word " forninst" it the damage
repairing;

So I mail my " remains" the crazed critic cre-
mated,

To let a true poet know how she was
" trated."

1884.

14

SOME OF WYOMING'S SINGERS.

TO DR J. T. DOYLE.

WIT's millionaire and princely son of Song,
  Whose palace stands remote from public gaze,
  All lighted up with culture's brilliant blaze,
In pleasure-grounds where Beauty's children
    throng,
And troops of fairies dance, nor deem it wrong;
  Where Fancy's silvery fountain freely plays,
  While splendid dreams adorn its flowering
    ways,
And Mirth keeps young, and Laughter hale and
    strong.

The wit whose lightning, flashed from theme to
    theme,
  Lays the bald mount of borrowed troubles
    bare;

While humor lights life's deeps with steadier
  gleam!
But when, like moonlight flood and starlight
  fair,
Their witching rays through Wisdom's case-
  ment stream,
The Muses, spellbound, bid farewell to Care!

TO THERON G. OSBORNE.

The singer's heart! the poet's speech!
No luscious thought beyond their reach,
  When Music spreads her wings;
And though the fruit too often be
But cherries ripe on Fancy's tree
(The bird we hear we seldom see),
  'Tis Philomel that sings!

But when this mood your heart enthralls,
It seems as though the music falls
  For Beauty's sake alone;

Your cherry-bird—the charming things!
With topknot cute and colored wings—
Drinks cherry wine and gayly sings,
   When Philomel has flown!

TO JOHN S. M^CGROARTY.

You sang at last so sweet a lay
   The Muse appeared before us,
And fairer than for many a day
   The heavenly hills hung o'er us!
With you, so gentle in her mien,
   So frank and unassuming,
Her pleasant smile and songful sheen
   Your every line illuming;
Her shell harmonious, in your hand,
   Has such bright heart-tints in it
That it reveals Truth's golden strand
   In one immortal minute!

TO E. A. NIVEN.

(Journalist.)

His prose is a swift and beautiful stream,
   The Song of the Brook recalls,
That dances along while others dream,
   And his songs are its water-falls!
With rapids here, and rapids there,
   For his muse's light canoe,
Who rides clear over the rocks of care
   When her shell goes shooting through!
Its shadow adrift in the shining tide,
   Till a cataract tumbles down,
When his muse, refreshed with her reckless
     ride,
   Strolls off to the nearest town,
With a twinkling smile, and a trace of tears,
   And the flowers she culled by the way;
But before she departs a poem appears
   That has something new to say.

July 1892.

THE ROBIN'S LAUGH.

WHEN I listened to your laughing,
  Robin, 'mid the barren boughs,
Then I heard remembered voices
  Ring through Love's deserted house,—
Voices sweet and void of sorrow,
  E'en as musical as yours:
Stay, blithe robin, lest I wrong you,
  Sounds like these the sad heart cures,
Sweet as childhood's cheeriest laughter,
  That no end to living sees!
Ah! you sing now, yet the song goes
  Laughing through the leafless trees.

If friends smile and call it dreaming,
  That you laugh before you sing,—

Yes, and laugh half through the singing
  And its after-echoing,—
Let them seek you out and listen,
  When they doubt the spring appears,
And they'll say no sweeter laughter
  Ever fell through happy tears!
Yet of sadness, when you've ended,
  E'en the happiest inly seize;
Robin, is not this the reason
  That you laugh through leafless trees?

Oh! Love's dwelling in the dingles
  Where the living laugh and sing,
And the light about their faces
  Glad with glimpses of the spring!
Where Love's voice is like the robin's,
  Rounded full and ripe with joy,
Rich in spring-like revelations
  For the youngest girl or boy!

Ah, Love! shall you hear in sadness
　　Autumn's merry-making breeze?
Then be this the only reason,
　　That she laughs through leafless trees.

April 19, 1884.

A FINE DAY.

THE day was so fine it impelled me to say it,
  Thus adding new zest to the joy it con-
    ferred,—
The new-born delight! 'twas a pleasure to
    weigh it
  On the scale of my voice with the weight of
    a word,
Then on that of the friends whom I met on my
    way,
With no scales on their eyes to discolor the
    day—
Fine day!————————————Fine day!

It is true, in the foulest of weather I've
    said it—
  Who hasn't? ha! ha! and felt foolish enough.
165

So different the day! in my long face you read it,
  Yet your answer was fine when it should
      have been rough.
"Fine day!" and I laughed as I went on my
    way,
And you smiled as you thought, what a funny
    fine day!

So vivacious I've been when the weather was
    vicious,
  My horizon so clear, though beclouded the
      sky,
That I shouted "Fine day!" and the fun was
    delicious
  When your ear-drum had hoodwinked the
      lens of the eye;
While you followed the hat the winds carried
    away,
From the stand-point I took 'twas a very fine
    day!

Too oft merely formal the day's salutations,
  Lacking feeling and warmth, though the
    weather is fair;
Weather-beaten must needs be our wise obser-
    vations,
  Yet one hearty "Good-morning!" may ward
    off despair.
Pleasant looks lend a charm to the least words
    we say;
It takes more than the weather to make a fine
    day.

So fine was that day when your fair one re-
    sponded,
  Which the fairer you knew not, the day or
    the maid!
With the drift of your speech the mild May-
    winds absconded,
  But the flower that she tossed you never shall
    fade.

Your " Fine day !" the May-winds caught up in
    their play;
'Twas the smile on her lips that perfected the
    day !

Fine day, ever fair in fond memory's keeping,—
    The day-old delight that you weighed with a
    word !
And now it is May with her merry eyes heap-
    ing
    Bright smiles on your head for the praise you
    conferred.
Then still keep repeating " Fine day !" and " Fine
    day !"—
The young, joyous June is the next one to
    weigh !
Good-day !————————————Good-day !

THE HOLY CHILD.

From lost Eden down the Seasons Four
    Had dreamed of the Holy Child;
Spring caught His smile in the dream's sweet
        core,
And in her heart hid it for evermore;
And her face thenceforth a sweeter look wore,
    And her spirit grew gentle and mild.
Every tree she touched broke out in blossoms
    That bloomed with a tenderer grace;
And a myriad bowers bared their white bosoms
    To make Him a resting-place!

From the Promise down the Seasons Four
    Had dreamed of the Birth Divine;
And Summer found, in the dream's deep core,
The Heart of her heart for evermore;

And redder thenceforth the roses she wore,
    And richer the fruit of the vine !
Then, flushed with the dream, round her pur-
        ple throne
    Her gifts of gold up-piled !
The royal honor seemed hers alone,
    To herald the Holy Child !

Through long ages dim the Seasons Four
    Had dreamed of His natal hour ;
And Autumn saw, in her sad dream's core,
The glorified look the young Child wore,
Though a dying heart in His bosom He bore,
And in her heart hid it for evermore
    In fading leaf and flower.
On flower and leaf a crimson glow
    Life out of death foretold !
And she said, " If He come ere winter winds
        blow,
    I will weave Him a crown of gold."

Down to His coming the Seasons Four
    Had dwelt on the Birth Divine;
Winter heard His voice when the dream was o'er,
And echoed its music for evermore.
And whiter thenceforth seemed the raiment she
    wore,
    And she cried, " The honor is mine:
I see His bright star through the frosty air
    gleam,
    Bending o'er Him, feel His warm breath;
And deep in my bosom I treasure the dream,
    Who had been the herald of Death."

Oh, heart of Winter with rapture thrilled,
    Thy dream, the first, came true!
With whitened locks the Seers of eld
The Blessed Babe in their arms had held;
But the human heart 'gainst the dream rebelled
    And the Lord of Glory slew!

Wise men of the East! how your golden gifts
glow
   In the light of Bethlehem's star!
As we carry bright gifts to our babes, through
the snow,
   Is its radiance near or far?

December 22, 1881.

MEMORIAL ODE.

(Read before the G. A. R. Post of Wilkesbarre, May 30, 1882.)

THE soldier's path, 'mid Hope's flushed flowers
    beginning,
  Ends here among the roses Love has strewn;
But then what lay between was worth the win-
    ning,
Though like Gehenna groaned the gory way
That led him to these tinted tents of May,
  And hence and upward to the fragrant camps
    of June—

And higher still t'wards Nature's highest
    heaven,
  Where light and sound the perfect day do
    make.

15*   173

Oh, happy slumberer! to thee 'tis given
To lie on Summer's heart and take thy rest,
Whether, like thee, in snow-white garment
    dressed
  For sleep, or watching 'mid the flowers till
    thou awake!

How like the mother, in her youthful beauty,
  She folds thee to her warm, sweet-smelling
    breast!
No longer thine to do a soldier's duty,
Helpless and happy here as any child,
To dreamland fair by countless blooms be-
    guiled,
  And all earth's sweets are thine without the
    weary quest!

But now do we, who have not yet divided
  The deep, dark waves that gave thee back
    thy youth,

Look o'er the waters where thy spirit glided
So like a dream unto this flowering shore
Where merry voices ring for evermore,
  Like children's voices, like thine own in sooth!

And some, thy friends who strayed with thee
    in childhood
  So oft these very burial-grounds among,
The golden meadows and the echoing wildwood,
With step like that of youth fresh garlands
    bring,
Bright as thine own hands wove in pleasant
    Spring,
  Till these old hearts of ours grow soft again
    and young.

Now far from us as thee, the noise of battle!
  Like babes upon a holiday at last
War's visage dim we scan, the cannon's rattle

Like them in wonder hear,—so old is peace!
This is not dotage,—'tis the heart's release
  From the long bondage of the grim and
    gloomy Past!

Gray veterans here there be, who carry flowers,—
  Would weep with strange delight if they
    might see
In vast array the hosts that once were ours!
Hailing once more in many a doubtful fight
The boys that saved the day, then sank from
    sight,—
  Would toss their hands and shout for joy
    hilariously.

Oh, Peace! what blessed boon is this you
    brought them
  That took the cruel sting of war away?
What charms Lethean, these you kindly
    wrought them

So well to heal the wounds that war had
   made ?
Oh, Peace! these hearts, once Sorrow's, dost
   pervade,
   What golden vistas down the Nation's larger
     day !

As May's white blossoms hide the hurts stern
   Winter
   Inflicted on the tempest-conquering trees,
That, like a cavalcade of heroes, enter
The rich realms where May was crownèd
   Queen ;
As earth's deep wounds are covered o'er with
   green,
   Your deathless deeds, O dead! and fadeless
     victories,

A brightening wilderness of blooms and glories,
   Loom up between us and the wrecks of war
m

And though we cherish still its touching stories,
Now, almost like romance, your sufferings
    seem
The blessed memories of a painful dream,
  Whose pain has given us Peace, as night the
    Morning Star!

Whose pangs have brought us joy, as night
    the golden morning;
  For not less brightly hath Aurora smiled,
That, as the legend saith, for her adorning
She stole full many a rosy child away;
  Nor Peace less bright, we cannot find to-
    day
    The flower of Chivalry unto her dawn beguiled!

Time hides the crimson of the cannonading,
  The imperial purple death did then display!
And war's red memories, faded now or fading,

Have yielded to the golden crown of Peace.
Let not her hopes, the while her powers
increase,
Like golden apples turn to ashes cold and
gray!

But living soldiers, not the less we love you;
Death yet denies you glory's tear-dewed
wreath;
Nor less ye love the Flag that soared above
you,
It firm refused to be your battle-shroud!—
Of this, surviving heroes, we are proud,
That Freedom's flowers blow fairer for your
loving breath!

Your voices, mingled with the battle's thunder
And feeble farewells of the dying brave,
Your hearts, that heard their heart-strings
break asunder,

Your hands, that clasped the hands that saved
 the day,
Your hands, that brought back laurels from
 the fray,
 Are needed the rich fruits of conflict yet to
 save !

Then let the buried dead again be buried
 Full deep beneath the flowers of Love and
 Peace !
Not as in war, when funeral rites were hurried,
But thoughtfully, and lovingly, and slow;
Ye have more time than in the long ago
 To scatter flowers, less cause the tear-drop to
 release !

Spare not the sweetest rose, the tenderest
 blossom
 Fond Nature into being ever fanned !
For martial garb she round each hero's bosom

Her "coat of many colors" loves to fold,
Helmeted with the daisy's sacred gold,
   To dull the darts that fly from Time's relent-
     less hand!

Sleep well beneath Columbia's starry skies!
   Your fame with hers coequal shall increase,
Ye soldier dead! Oh, may your sacrifice
   To deeds as grand our souls bestir, in peril-
     ous peace!

THE VANISHED MAIDEN.

THE gold in the sky was burning,
  As I walked one eve by the sea,
And the lustre it shed was turning
  All things into gold but me ;
For wrapped in a mantle of sorrow,
  I was proof 'gainst the beautiful change,
And my soul was unable to borrow
  That glory so silent and strange.

But soon, with a music enchanted,
  That rose from the shells on the shore,
With a phantom of joy I was haunted,
  And I heard her soft whisper once more,—
The voice of my own vanished maiden,
  Buried deep in the caves of the sea,
And my soul then sighed for her Aiden,
  And fluttered—with her to be free !
182

The music increased, and the billows
　　Fell back into deep repose,
With white tranquil foam for their pillows,
　　When a form from the waters arose ;
'Twas the form of my long-lost maiden,
　　Buried deep in the caves of the sea,
Whose soul had returned from her Aiden
　　To talk for one moment with me.

" Let grief from your bosom be banished,
　　Be happy on earth for awhile,
For soon the maid that has vanished
　　Will welcome you there with a smile,
Where the gold in the sky is burning,
　　And whence we shall look on the waves,
While the lustre that's shed is turning
　　All things into gold but our graves."

July 21, 1879.

GOD AND THE SEA.

"And his weary eyes welcome the sight of the sea."—*Blaine's Despatch.*

FROM that death-haunted chamber they solemnly
bore him,
  To die in their arms it might be!
But strong-wingèd angels flew seaward before
him,
To move the great heart of the deep to restore him,
Rouse, nourish, and rest him, breathe through
him and o'er him
  The blood-thrilling balm of the sea,—
  The life-giving breath and the strength of
the sea.

Stern Science grew motherly, thoughtful, and
tender
  As his own loving mother might be!
184

And day and night pondered how best she
    could render
Assistance, so naught merely human would
    hinder
The brave heart in that body so pallid and
    slender
    From sounding its thanks to the sea,—
    From trilling its drum-beats of joy by the
    sea.

The face of young Autumn was flushed as with
    fever,
    And crimson as Summer's might be !
And her touch was so scorching they scarce
    could believe her
Sweet Autumn to be ; yet she was no de-
    ceiver,—
Our burden of sorrow seemed greatly to grieve
    her,

And she raved in that run to the sea ;

But at sunset she smiled,—the fair bride of

the sea !

That day through fair Autumn's delusion he

dallies

With dreams of a blessing to be !

Though nature is drooping, the President ral-

lies,

And they run a rapider rate through the val-

leys,

And the good engine glides down the hill-tops

and sallies

Forth of woodlands, fast nearing the sea,

Till "his weary eyes welcome the sight of

the sea."

Yet gently and tenderly thither they bore him ;

To die was not heaven's decree,

For the swift-wingèd angels flew seaward before
him,

And stirred the great heart of the deep to restore him,

Nurse, nourish, and rest him, breathe through
him and o'er him

The life-giving breath of the sea,

And he gains! by the grace of our God and
His sea!

September 9, 1881.

AT GARFIELD'S GRAVE.

BENEATH that grand triumphal arch the night,
  O'erlaid with fading stars in lieu of flowers,
  Fit tokens of this fleeting life of ours,
A warrior passed, so altered to the sight,
Men said had won a world in valiant fight;
  When a voice answered from the King's high
     towers :
  "Two worlds hath won, the wreck of Eden's
     bowers
And the new Eden death can never smite."

Tall archways, eloquent with flowers, arise;
  Triumphal music beats its anguished breast,

Then breathes a requiem caught from sacred
    choirs ;
Kind eyes look out, like stars, from sorrow's
    skies,
    And pour their love-light round his place
    of rest.
Sweet starlight left of Eden's lingering fires I

September 28, 1881.

LOVE'S WOUNDS.

LIFE the first-born of Eden's bowers, Death
    last,
  And Love that came between,—mysterious
    Three!
  O Life and Death, at last on which of ye
Shall blame of Love's unkindest hurts be
    cast?
All healèd then, and every sorrow passed,
  Whose pitying hand, whose balsam-dropping
    tree
Left for those wounds and all that misery
The sweetest cordial? Death's the icono-
    clast?
O Life, I fear Love at the last will say
  That thou, not Death, did most severely
    smite!

And tell how, when he faint and bleeding lay
By Time's roadside, Death softened at the
    sight,
And decently enwrapping him in white,
Took all the soreness from his wounds away,

February 22, 1882.

BURIED LOVE'S EPITAPH.

KIND words, warm as Love's heart, Love's
  living breath,
  In marble cold and white! A subtle flame
  Within whose charmèd circle one dear name
Defieth the devouring jaws of Death!
Not heeding what the night wind muttereth,
  Smiling through storm and sunshine just the
    same,
  In this lone shelter, more secure than fame,
Content with what surviving Love's heart
    saith.
The marble's time-swept snow may drift away,
  Or mingle with the dust that sleeps below;
  But in its stead sweet flowers shall rise, and so
Suggest the fragrance of her name, decay

Can never touch, and when the last flower
  dies,

Heaven will reveal Love's name, Love's voice,
  Love's eyes!

February 2, 1882.

1   *n*   17

THE RICH AND THE SUFFER-
ING.

Has she, indeed, red rose so fresh and fair,
  Journeyed far up the valley of the night
Unto these purpling hills of morn ?   Is there
  No faintness in thy heart and on thy
    sight ?
Is't fear, still lingering, makes thee tremble so ;
  This flush a vaporish fever in thy blood ?
Nay, nay, it was the breeze.   Why, do you
    know
  I feel as bright as any new-blown bud.

Yet couldst thou tell what thou hast seen and
    heard :
  What grim and ghastly shapes beset thy
    way,

What moanings in the dark, no pity stirred,

    What voices praying for the dawn of day!

I fear the joy thy greeting now bestows

Would turn to pain, though passing fair thou

    be, rich rose!

June 13, 1881.

HENRY W. LONGFELLOW.

WHAT birds, the bards of air, in singing say,
    Whisper the roses, and his ruddy Muse,
When poets born behold the break of day,
    Music, like manna, mingles with the dews.

Exhaling, as the measures grow in might,
    This early fragrance from the fields of song;
How have we quaffed its lyrical delight,
    His fancy's goodly company among!

How reddened all the East of our desire
    With song-beams from this singer's glowing
        breast!
A grateful age will greet whose fadeless fire
    In gleams of gold athwart its fadeless West.

196

The wilds of nature, when his music came,
   Hailed in its sheen their mysteries unveiled;
While woods and waters, and their hosts, by
     name,
   And all the winds, its shaping spirit hailed.

It lures some peeping glory from a star,
   Shows deeper pathos in a pining flower,
And, like a leaven of all sweet sounds there are,
   Imbues with rapture many a lonely hour.

Poems pure as the dreams of Paradise
   Fair innocence finds lingering in her heart,
The sun's white hands that bathe her waking
     eyes,
   The gifts they bring, the color they impart.

Whose death-defying harmony inspires
   A listener's throb of triumph in one's breast;
And imagery refulgent as the fires
   The poet-sun transfigures in the West.

As when of old had vanished all the dews,
  The manna and its memory yet remained;
The first fresh flush of fancy loath to lose,
  What   treasures   hath   this   faithful   singer
    gained !

What treasures on his fellows hath bestowed !
  And not the lays alone for which we yearned,
But   when   the   suns   were   set   that   on   them
    glowed,
  The   strength   imparted   and   the   lessons
    learned.

Filled with a melody, the Golden Rule
  Is waking in the world, beside his own;
He breathes more beauty on the beautiful,
  Or leaves new loveliness where it had flown.

His tender songs stir pity's fount of tears,
  Grief's   bursting   drops   of   balm   break   out
    between,

As sunshine in an April shower appears,
  To turn the wastes of winter into green.

A guide by journeyings heavenward glorified!
  Pointing to cold and sullen steeps, that freeze
Ambition's breath, leads, down the mountain-
    side,
  Where summer strives for Summer's purple
    ease.

Held by her sun-browned hand, and not a
    dream,
  A golden ladder leans against the sky,
And joins two worlds which very distant seem
  Until the bright ascent our spirits try.

Poesy, radiant in the twilight dim
  That on the longest life comes unawares,
At night will give good angels charge of him
  Whose earthly harp so much resembles theirs.

But oh! while yet the hues of eve remain,
  Silence may sepulchre some matchless ode;
The fragment of a psalm, one sweet refrain,
  If heard, her heart with joy were overflowed.

Ultima Thule his moist eyes have descried,
  Its quiet voices echo to his quest—
Sad sounds, like farewells, in his last songs tide
  Soft to her saddened soul the poet's sigh for
    rest.

February 14, 1881.

THE VISION OF COLUMBUS.

Is that fire on the dark horizon reflected from
    land or sea?
A will-o'-the-wisp of the waters or the glory
    about to be?
A sudden enchantment falls on a sleepless and
    watchful crew;
Yet twice had they shouted " Land !" with never
    a shore in view.

Columbus kneels in his cabin, his soul in thanks
    outpoured
For the vision that comes to the victor, and
    a sign vouchsafed by the Lord.
Had he seen in the midnight glimmer of a
    sleep-enveloped strand
The smile of his life's ideal, with a crucifix in
    her hand?

Could it be that his soul's belovèd, the be-
    trothed of a deathless dream,
Had caught from her outermost Eden his cara-
    vels' distant gleam ?
But as yet not one of the doubters of a day
    or two before
Has demanded the velvet doublet, as the first
    to descry the shore.

And whence that shadowy splendor, with a cry
    of " Land !" on his lips,
Like the gleam of Isabel's jewels in the midst
    of the booming ships ?
Can it be the spirit of Isabel, the form of his
    royal friend,
In the jewels of joy resplendent, in a dream of
    his journey's end ?

He knows that once in the voyage her shadow
    shimmered between

The blades of a crew rebellious and the friend
    of the Spanish queen.
The veil from the dark sea lifted, its ghostly
    gulf explored!
The dragon of Superstition pierced by Dis-
    covery's sword!

He has waged and won the battle that waited
    a thousand years
For its Genoese commander and the gleam of
    its Spanish spears.
He has seen all the shadows of fear from the
    island of Ferro flee,
And the wounded roc fall limp in the sweep
    of a wider sea;

The dreams that are medieval, like the mists
    of night, dissolve
In the swirl of the smiling waters when the
    world begins to revolve!

He has waged and won the battle, in the face
    of forlorn surprise,
In the menace of murderous madness that
    glared from a hundred eyes,

In the face of swords that pointed to soundings
    that tell no tales,—
With the faith that overcometh and the courage
    that never fails !
With a faith whose glance auroral his men to
    themselves revealed,
With the truth that the victory winneth when
    Rescue has fled the field:

With a faith, in the climax of terror, that stood
    for those trembling tars
In imminent stead for the comfort that fled
    from the sun and the stars !
Every man of his crew forgiven for a menace
    of more than death,

For they sailed, by the chart of Columbus and
    the Trade-wind's bewildering breath,

At a speed whose persistence appalled them,
    'neath a canopy far too fair,
Its sunrise the doom of the dreamer, its sun-
    set the dream of despair!
Sailing on forever, they feared, with a menace
    in every mile,
On a sea with a face as smooth as its dragon's
    reflected smile;

Inspired by the man they hated, losing heart
    but to hate him the more;
His will, like the winds that drove them,
    whether shipwreck! or sea! or shore!
His will, like the winds that held them, head-
    ing away to the West,
Uniform, constant, and changeless as the love
    in a father's breast.

Had he heard in that midnight vision, in a
    moment of joy profound,
The ghost of the Inquisition confess that the
    earth is round?
Did he see on the brow of Arragon the shadow
    of lasting regret,
To be found in a time of trouble the friend
    who would fain forget?

The look of ineffable rapture on the features of
    proud Castile,
To find the ocean furrowed by Christianity's
    faithful keel?
Was John of Portugal present, with the mien
    of a moody king,
To write on the chart of Columbus " Remorse"
    with his royal ring?

Remorse for the terms rejected, the treasures
    he lost for aye!

The ten years lost to Columbus, and a waiting
    world's delay!
"Ha! ha!" cry the coming squadrons, hidalgos
    in quest of gold,
On highways, for ages dreaded, where the
    waves of the dark sea rolled!

To Genoa's foremost freeman, commissioned of
    God and Spain,
Did the skies' starry Dream of Columbia shed
    more splendor than man could explain?
In the vision vouchsafed the victor who nobly
    fulfils his vow
Could he see the centuries wreathing the fade-
    less leaf for his brow?

Had he touched on the time enchanted when
    childhood lisped his name,
And Isabel's friend, Columbus, every school-
    boy's hero became?

Had he noted the compass he conquered, the
    needle he shaped to his mind,
In a tremor of precious rapture for the paths
    that were yet to find?

It matters not who the finders; for the least
    and the greatest of these,
From the world that is round, he has wrested
    the secrets of all the seas!
But in lieu of his princely titles behold his
    fame assured
In the unwritten terms of the treaty and the
    treasures that Time secured!

What a lesson his pageant teaches, whose
    triumph was far too brief!
What a picture of greatness shrouded in the
    shadows of shame and grief!
But lo! when the fetters were stricken from
    Isabel's faithful friend,

What a symbol for progress and freedom and
the triumph of truth in the end!

The ages to come will bless him, as ages gone
by have blessed,

For the wealth the world has discovered with
his Eastern wand in the West!

For the wand that borrowed its magic from his
dazzling dream of the East,

Till the dawn of knowledge deepened and the
wisdom of men increased!

Fair, phantom sail Santa Maria, forerunner of
Liberty's ships,

Usher in the Columbian Era, with thy cap-
tain's cry on its lips!

Let the realms that the Pinta announces re-
spond to Humanity's Dream,

Till the Niña, the need of the nations, has an-
chored in Liberty's Stream.

October 10 and 11, 1892.

18*